BLACK DAY AT HANGDOG

When exiled bank robber Moses Kane arrives in Haven's Hangdog Saloon, he is accompanied by deadly gunslingers and a lust for revenge. Old-timer Wilf Gannon smells trouble, for the canyon town is cut off by flood waters and it seems nothing can save the dying town's ageing inhabitants. But, beyond Twin Bluffs Pass, rancher Adam Flint is concerned for Gannon, Mort Baxter wants his money, and the Sioux Long Arrow wants Kane . . .

Books by Jack Sheriff
in the Linford Western Library:

BURY HIM DEEP IN TOMBSTONE
THE MAN FROM THE STAKED PLAINS
INCIDENT AT POWDER RIVER

JACK SHERIFF

BLACK DAY AT HANGDOG

Complete and Unabridged

LINFORD
Leicester

First published in Great Britain in 1999 by
Robert Hale Limited
London

First Linford Edition
published 2001
by arrangement with
Robert Hale Limited
London

British Library CIP Data

Sheriff, Jack
  Black day at Hangdog.—Large print ed.—
Linford western library
1. Western stories
2. Large type books
I. Title
823.9′14 [F]

ISBN 0–7089–5924–5

Published by
F. A. Thorpe (Publishing)
Anstey, Leicestershire

Set by Words & Graphics Ltd.
Anstey, Leicestershire
Printed and bound in Great Britain by
T. J. International Ltd., Padstow, Cornwall

This book is printed on acid-free paper

1

As far as old Wilf Gannon could work out on the chill night Ben Stone put the question to him in the Hangdog Saloon, Haven had begun to die round about the time Red Cloud rode his pony down to Fort Laramie and signed away his people's future. The two events were in no way connected, but with Ben having been up the Bozeman around the treaty time Wilf knew the remark would jolt some memories and, maybe, put a spark into conversation that was about as lively as damp kindling.

'End of '68,' Ben agreed now. 'Close on fifteen years ago.' He scratched his ragged thatch of grey hair and behind wire-framed spectacles his tired, watery-blue eyes stared into some far distance. Across the table from him, Hank Travis trickled smoke towards the old brass lamp that was flickering as it swung lazily above the table and nodded sagely.

'Cruellest winter I ever saw,' he said in his lazy Texan drawl, talking through teeth clamped on his thin cheroot and concentrating hard as he tipped the whiskey bottle over his glass with a big scarred hand that was pretty steady for almost midnight. Straggly grey hair flopped over his lined forehead as he went on, 'I'd rode up from Amarillo with a rancher drivin' a herd up to Montana and damn near froze to death. Vowed then I'd head back to the Nueces in the spring, but I never did get paid and one thing led to another . . . the way things do.'

'If you put it that way,' John Darling said, 'this darned place has been dyin' ever since folks was led to believe there was gold in these hills, realized they'd been fooled and ran that crazy Forty-niner out of town. In twelve months most of those chased him out had seen sense and hightailed after him — and

2

the only place we've been led since then is downhill at a gallop.'

He collected the empty bottle off the table, stood up and stomped out of the shifting pool of light and round behind the bar, a portly man with bright red galluses stretched across the shoulders of his collar-less white shirt, and thin strands of what had once been dark hair plastered across a pink scalp shiny with sweat.

When he returned, wiping dust and clogged spiders' webs off a fresh bottle with the hem of the white apron that was stretched to bursting around his ample middle, he was met by a fierce gust of cold, damp air as Dan Ford stumbled in over the threshold and struggled to shut the door against the wind's strength while slapping rain off his hat and blowing through his drooping white moustache like a riled old bronc.

'I admire this man,' Wilf Gannon said, keeping his seamed face straight as the others chuckled at the newcomer's discomfort. 'Lives in a goddamn ghost town, yet pins on his tarnished badge and does the rounds every night just to protect us from the hordes of outlaws waitin' to pounce and rob us of our hard-earned dollars — '

'Ain't nobody doin' any pouncin' on a night like this,' Dan Ford cut in, ''less it's a half-drowned alley cat workin' to reduce the rat population. Four-legged, that is. And,' he continued, swinging his slicker off his bony shoulders to a raucous chorus of protests as icy rainwater showered the drinkers, 'if you don't break open that bottle, John, you'll be lookin' for a new town constable because the one you've got'll've froze to death.'

'Or been demoted clear out of sight,' John Darling said, grinning. He splashed whiskey into a fresh glass, watched with satisfaction as Ford tossed it back with a grimace that could have been pleasure but was more likely the pain of a blistered gullet. 'Dan, you're the only man I ever met started off as US marshal and in the space of a town's living and dying worked his way right back down to the bottom of the rubbish heap.'

'Which remark paints a pretty grim picture of this settlement,' Dan Ford said. 'John, you and Bonnie scratch a living out of this excuse for a drinking den and the mercantile next door. Hank's lucky to see half-a-dozen horses a week pass through his livery stable — and, yes, Ben, I know; you and Jenny ain't seen that many people in your rooming-house in more'n a year.' He shook his head, marvelling. 'About the only one of us with any sense is Wilf . . . ' And here he raised his glass in a mocking toast. 'Old Wilf there, he passes every day without raisin' a sweat because he knows — '

'From long experience,' Wilf said mildly.

'Because he knows — from long experience — that in this purty little town called Haven, there ain't a goddamn thing worth doing.'

5

'I remember once,' John Darling mused, 'Haven was such a fine place to live some wag took a running iron, rode out a ways and inserted an E after the H on the town sign.'

'Wasn't more than a year after that he worked on it again,' Ben Stone pointed out. 'Crossed out that E, stuck on a final T and added two little words that neatly summed up our prospects.'

'Haven't A Hope,' Wilf said. 'It's still there — and we still ain't got one. And if I remember, Ben, that wag was you.'

Ben Stone nodded. 'That hunk of wood's the only thing I've put a brand on in more than ten years. Did it three months after I bust my leg ropin' a steer . . . ' He fumbled in his pocket for his tobacco sack, and in his face there was a despairing anger that settled over the table like a dusty shroud.

About then Wilf dragged out his silver turnip watch, saw it was gone midnight and climbed out of his chair to walk in the laboured way dictated by his game hip over to the window and peer out across the expanse of muddy street. He had to scrub the condensation with the edge of his hand to do it, winced as he saw the curtain of rain sweeping down the steep slope and across the single lantern swinging in front of Ben and Jenny's rooming-house, and turned away from the window with a disgusted grunt.

Near to winter on the south side of the Bighorn, Wyoming Territory. A chill in the air hanging beneath ragged, wind-torn clouds leaking a steady rain. Sensible men would be at home in bed. The only ones caught out in this weather would be drifters with nowhere to go, or the hard, restless men who rode the wild trails one step ahead of the law.

Wilf's boot heels clomped unevenly on the rough boards as he limped across to the old pot-bellied stove, tossed in a couple of resiny pine logs and slammed the door with a clang. Sparks hissed up the battered flue. A tendril of smoke curled, its tang catching Wilf's nostrils, stinging his mild grey eyes.

He blinked, faced back down the room, eased his shoulders, then wandered reluctantly away from the stove's warmth, thick fingers fumbling in his shirt pocket for his tobacco sack.

Over at the table, Dan Ford had finally got his slicker hooked over the back of his chair, doffed his Stetson to expose a shiny bald scalp, and sat down. John Darling tipped out the greasy pack of cards, and for several seconds the only sound to be heard above the moaning wind was the rhythmic snapping as Hank dealt the first hand of a poker game that would likely see them all the way through the next hour, and most of the way through the next bottle of whiskey.

With his colleagues' warmth tended to, Wilf settled down on the long seat up against the window. He pushed aside an ashtray and tossed the makings onto the small table, took time fashioning a cigarette; snapped a match, applied it, watched the smoke spiral away in the cold, swirling draught.

Not a man among them wasn't closer to sixty than fifty, he ruminated — and that included himself, only he was looking back over his shoulder from the increasingly lonely high ground he wryly talked of as being above the snow line. Most mornings it took every one of them ten minutes just to roll out of bed and stretch the kinks out of their joints. Each day crawled past without incident. Every night they ended up here; had done for . . . oh, more years than Wilf cared to count.

So John Darling was right: Haven had commenced dying before it was halfway built — a cluster of houses and false-fronted business establishments erected towards the top end of a deep canyon that was sheltered by tall pines clinging to its high steep slopes and damn near cut off from the outside world at its lower end by Twin Bluffs Pass, a couple of immense, sheer-sided cliffs flanking a wide, dry river-bed that

9

allowed entry to the canyon for a man on horseback — maybe even a top-buggy at a pinch — but not a lot more.

In bad weather, a tough beaver would have trouble.

The town owed its existence to a crazy miner's dream of finding gold, and the zealous newspaperman who had listened to his imaginings and spread the word. Before the ink was dry on his story, more than a thousand men had ridden in beneath the tall bluffs; hard men, desperate men, the weak and the curious, the speculators and gamblers. With them came honest businessmen, shrewd enough to recognize a need and figure, rightly, that there was more money to be made from meeting that need than ever came from digging holes in a barren hillside.

But even they recognized that the town was built on a dream. And when that dream died, the town of Haven — which had never aspired to anything grander than raw timber frames nailed into shape and covered with tar paper by greedy men going nowhere in a hurry — had nothing to sustain it. The small outlying ranches to the south — Adam Flint's Circle F, Jade Winston's Lazy J — took the bulk of their limited trade to the nearest big town and came to Haven for necessities — reluctantly, and not often enough. The loaded emigrant wagons lumbering towards California passed by further north along the Bozeman or the Oregon. Those that did stray south drove past with ragged kids hanging out the back and a scrawny man up on the seat with his tired eyes fixed on another distant dream.

Or did do, Wilf reminded himself wistfully; with the coming of the railroad those wagons had gone the way of the buffalo.

But all men have their dreams, Wilf thought, half listening to the murmur of conversation in the Hangdog and staring blind at the glowing tip of his cigarette. His own had been shattered when a two-year drought wiped out his small herd of milking cows. The sheer heartache of it killed his wife and the only thing left for him was to sell up and move into town.

That had been well before Haven lay down and turned up its toes; and for a long time, after the haunting loneliness of his deserted spread where the creaking windmill kept him awake nights cruelly reminding him of what he had lost, the warmth and gruff compassion he had discovered in this circle of fine friends had been his salvation.

Their compassion had come from long practice at healing raw wounds.

Even now there were gaps in what Wilf knew of the others. Ben Stone was a cowhand fallen on bad times who had teamed up with a pretty schoolmarm who had come West with ambitions and finished up running a rooming-house.

John Darling had built the saloon and adjoining mercantile with his own hands — the first businessman to arrive in Haven, and always the one most likely to succeed.

In the first place he had provided what every man who came to Haven needed: supplies of one kind or another to maintain their bid for the rich prizes they were convinced lay buried on the slopes, and the strong drink they would turn to either to celebrate a strike, or to drown their sorrows.

But John Darling was also backed by a strong woman. Bonnie Darling, daughter of an itinerant Bible puncher, had married the young businessman and settled easily into the rough life on the Great Plains. But she had been less happy about the move to Haven, and some friction had developed between her and John when he stubbornly refused to move from a town that had lost its way.

Wilf recalled how, in his own loneliness, he had from time to time allowed himself to read a deeper meaning into the warm glances the dissatisfied Bonnie Darling bestowed on him. But that was as far as it had gone, and that was the way it remained.

Dan Ford had wound up carrying a badge — but where he'd come from, nobody could say. Likewise it seemed pretty certain that Hank Travis had been a wrangler back in his home state and had come north with a cattle drive; but there were those who had witnessed his prowess with a six-gun, when Haven was awash with footloose drifters and salty hellions, who were apt to be sceptical and offer their own theories on his background — when he was well out of earshot!

But even a gunslinger — if that was what he had been — loses his edge, and maybe to a man with enemies lurking along his back-trail Haven had appeared like a godsend.

Well, no matter where they'd come from, they'd all stayed, scratching a living in one way or another and waiting . . . but if you were to grab hold of them and ask them what exactly they were waiting for, well . . .

Wilf killed the cigarette, and grinned

14

ruefully. He made enough money to see him through the winters by driving the chuck wagon for Adam Flint, and dishing up hot meals for the Circle F punchers. A long way down the trail from owning his own spread, but, hell, a man —

He blinked, jerked rudely out of his thoughts as the Hangdog's doors burst open, banging back against the wall and letting in another icy blast of wind and rain. The lantern over the table swung wildly, playing cards lifted and flew in the crazily flickering light like frosted winter leaves — and Wilf always reckoned, when they looked back on it, that it was Hank Travis who yelled out, 'Either come in or stay out, mister, but for Christ's sake shut that goddamn door!'

Then, as the doors slammed to, shutting out the storm, they were all stunned into silence. Five elderly men turned blank faces to stare at the tall, gaunt man dressed in rain-soaked black clothing who stood dripping onto the sawdust-sprinkled boards.

The face was high of cheekbone, square of jaw; there was some Mex in there, maybe a lot more white man, but none of it any good.

And what they stared at most of all were the glittering, steel-grey eyes that squinted at them from beneath the soggy brim of the concho studded hat, and the twin six-guns that jutted like striking rattlers from holsters lashed with rawhide thongs to the man's lean thighs.

2

Six miles south of Haven the icy rain driven by fierce winds sweeping in off the vast expanse of open prairie drove the three slickered riders back under the trees. They urged their mounts deep into the woods, plunging through the crackling undergrowth to put a thick barrier of oaks between them and the storm before sliding from shiny wet saddles and hurriedly building a fire on the dry earth beneath a towering, rocky outcrop.

A tall, bone-thin man with wide shoulders and a wayward left eye that gleamed milkily in the darkness, coughed harshly in the billowing clouds of acrid smoke, swung a savage kick at a mossy rock and called angrily, 'I sure as hell hope you know what you're doin', Streak.'

The powerful man with long, white-streaked black hair tied in a thick ponytail finished lashing his slicker behind the big blue roan's saddle, strode towards the fire and spat into the crackling flames.

'*I* sure as hell hope I know what I'm doin', Slim,' he said. 'Twice over.' And firelight glinted on strong white teeth as his unshaven face split in a mirthless grin. 'Because if I'm wrong on the first count, that posse of irate ranchers and townsfolk ain't ridin' like the wind in a southerly direction like we hope it is.' He swung around as twigs crackled underfoot, said softly, 'If I'm wrong on both, then Haven ain't like I remember it, and we could be in trouble.'

He was in his late forties, the man called Streak, wearing a drab brown coat over a faded work shirt, black pants tucked into stovepipe boots. The immediate impression he gave the casual onlooker was one of power, a raw, primitive presence that in the meek would perhaps inspire awe. But the more observant would catch glimpses of wildness in the dark eyes, of an unnerving unpredictability, and they would know — these observant men — that those were characteristics that meant a man could never be trusted, and so rather than awe they would begin to feel fear.

The third man stomped past, swearing under his breath. He'd come stumbling back out of the dripping woods and now hunkered down, a stocky man with slicker swept back as he rigged a branch over the fire and suspended a blackened coffee pot full of spring water in the dancing flames.

'Streak, we were in trouble soon's that Indian talked you into turning our backs on the New Mexico border.' He straightened as he swung away from the fire, slapping his filthy hands on his pants, and there was outrage in his weak, watery-blue eyes.

'So what the hell's that make you, Frank? When we piled out of that bank you was with us. If you didn't agree to the change of plan all you had to do was take your share and head south. Ain't no damn use complainin' when we've crossed half of Wyoming Territory.'

Frank Tighe spat savagely, his eyes flicking pointedly to the two bulky sacks hanging heavy against the big roan's flanks.

'Maybe we ought to do that right now,' he said, 'before you get us bogged down in a backwoods box-canyon, one way in, no way out, and a posse settin' there waitin' for us to pop out with the spring thaw.'

Dakota Slim laughed flatly, dragged the makings out of his shirt pocket, began fashioning a cigarette with stiff, cold fingers.

'Frank, you know damn well Streak's wrong on his first count. That posse's been trackin' us for more'n a week, you head back down the trail those *hombres*'ll be so all fired mean they won't bother askin' questions.'

He used his thumbnail to flick a match, his wayward eye gleaming white through its flare as he went on bluntly,

'But that means we ain't got no choice. We walked into their bank and stole the cash they had put by to see them over winter, so we do this Streak's way, or die at the end of a rope. Django Orr's rode ahead to take care of any law. That Sioux kid, Young Fox, is watchin' his back. If Streak's remembrance is right,' — and here he glowered at the big man — 'the goddamn place is a ghost town run by a bunch of harmless old-timers — and once we're in, there ain't no posse going to hang around all winter.'

The pot rattled, spilling steam and hissing droplets of water into the smoke and flames as Streak, whistling tunelessly through his teeth, bent to remove the lid with his gloved hand and toss in a handful of coffee. Frank Tighe huddled forwards towards the heat, blue eyes narrowed, face sullen in the flickering light.

Away from the fire, Dakota Slim cupped the glowing cigarette in his palm. His head was cocked as he looked off into the woods, listening, thoughts inward, eyes unseeing. He was a loner, Dakota Slim, a man who had ridden out of the Badlands with a blank past and a future he had been heard to describe, with the grim philosophy of the outlaw gun, as beginning afresh with each sunrise. The wayward eye was the result of a knife wound that had left a livid scar from that eye's corner back through the thick dark hair over his left ear and down to the nape of the neck. The effect of the two deformities was to create a countenance that would scare the hell out of a man on a dark night, and in broad daylight give him the urge — when he saw Slim approaching — to cross the street or duck into the nearest doorway.

'Let's see if I've got this right,' Frank Tighe said softly, talking into the flames. 'Orr went in maybe an hour ago, making for the Hangdog. Young Fox peeled off, went in back of the livery stable, stays out of sight — on no account shows his face.'

Streak came alongside Dakota Slim,

nudged his elbow, and the lean man turned, took the steaming mug of coffee.

'We give 'em two hours,' Streak said to Tighe. 'If Young Fox ain't hammered back down here like a hoss with its tail on fire, we figure Django Orr's bellied up against that bar, nice and snug, and we follow them in.'

Softly, disbelievingly, Dakota Slim said, 'Streak, that kid Young Fox talked you into this, but you ain't seen the place since a crazy old miner got rode out of town on his mule and an interferin' do-gooder took away your squaw. Not knowin' what's awaitin' us, I reckon those must be the cockeyedest tactics ever dreamed up by a man supposed to have all his senses in the right place.'

Streak's grin was wolfish.

'Maybe,' he said. 'But if anyone's in danger, it surely ain't me.'

★　★　★

The bunched horses rattled across the yard, coming out of the sweeping rain into the circle of light in a jingling, jostling pack of lathered hide, gleaming leather and slick yellow oilskin. Vapour from the blowing horses and the steaming hides of animals and men drifted like smoke in the swinging lamplight. Weapons jutted from gunbelts and saddle boots. From beneath limp, dripping hat brims, black eyes glittered out of drawn, unshaven faces.

The lead rider lifted a hand, drew rein. As tired horses milled in confusion behind him and bunkhouse doors creaked open spilling more light into the yard, he swung down heavily, an aching weariness evident in the wooden stiffness of his solid legs, the slump of broad shoulders. He dragged a battered Stetson off a coarse thatch of grey hair, beat rainwater from it against a scarred timber upright as he stomped up onto the worn board gallery.

'Mort, you taken to ridin' out in the night rain?'

Mort Baxter gripped the bony hand of the gaunt man who came out of the ranch house to meet him, eased his shoulders stiffly, was half aware of another, sinewy man moving purposefully across the rain-swept yard behind him.

'Not out of pleasure,' he growled. 'Adam, my boys would sure appreciate hot coffee, something to fill empty bellies . . . the use of one of your lofts for the night . . . '

'Glad of the company,' Adam Flint said. He nodded to the rangy man now waiting at the foot of the steps and, as Mort Baxter followed the tall rancher into the house, Mexican spurs jingling, he heard Flint's foreman issuing directions and mounts being wheeled about, the gruff, relieved laughter of weary men looking forward to hot food and a bed of sweet dry straw.

The room was long and low, heated by a blazing log fire in a massive stone grate, and lit by hanging oil lamps that shone on dark wood furniture and scattered animal skins. The harsh wind was a muted whisper outside the thick walls, the tinkle of bottle against glass a welcome sound as Adam Flint poured two stiff drinks.

'All right, let's hear it,' he said, handing Baxter a glass and watching with obvious satisfaction as the trail-weary rancher took a first, appreciative drink. 'Half a dozen armed men ride into my yard, eyes like holes poked in snow, horses ragged, wrung-out. Couple of small ranchers, one feller I know for sure owns a mercantile. That stinks of posse, Mort.'

Baxter nodded, lips pursed as he gazed into his glass. 'Four men entered Colorado some miles south of Cheyenne,' he said, and the grey eyes that lifted to meet Flint's were smouldering with old anger. 'Rode into town, tied up outside the bank. When they unhitched and rode back out no more than ten minutes later, they left two good men gut-shot, took most of a town's hard-earned cash.'

'And headed through the mountains towards the New Mex border,' Flint said, 'as they always do.' He lifted an eyebrow. 'So what the hell are you and your men doing riding north through Wyoming towards the Bighorns, Mort?'

Baxter sighed, pushed blunt fingers through his wiry black hair, absently massaged the back of his neck.

He had served in the 1st Texas Cavalry alongside Adam Flint through the last bitter months of the Civil War, and the two men had kept the friendship going into the troubled peace even though they had gone their separate ways. Now, Mort Baxter ran a big beef herd on several thousand sprawling acres in northern Colorado, a good 200 miles to the south of where Adam Flint had established the Circle F between the Powder and Crazy Woman Creek in Wyoming Territory.

On occasions the two men would find themselves attending the same Cattlemen's Association meeting in one part of the country or another, and at such times they enjoyed sharing a drink. But those days were becoming less frequent, and so Baxter felt considerable annoyance at the thought that it had needed a hard, gruelling manhunt to bring about one of their rare meetings, and that the talk now should be taken with the deeds of violent men.

'Well, I tell you, Adam,' Baxter said ruminatively, 'for a while the reasoning behind their flight north had every damn one of us stumped.'

He caught the sack of Bull Durham tossed his way by Flint, hitched his backside onto the arm of a chair to roll a smoke while the lean rancher replenished the glasses.

'Then,' Baxter continued, 'three days out, Lake, the feller owns the mercantile, he finally clamped his teeth on the name that had been dancin' out of reach on the end of his tongue. From then on it was a matter not of following those outlaws, but of taggin' along behind and seein' if they went where we already knew they were goin' — if you see what I mean.'

He twisted the end of the quirly, stuck it in his mouth and grinned cheerfully at Adam Flint.

Flint grunted, snapped a match, lit Baxter's cigarette.

'What name?' he said flatly.

'Moses Kane.'

Flint swore. 'Streak. Man who owned Haven before that crazy miner hollered gold and pulled in half the world.'

'Adam, that man *was* Haven. Built himself a cabin backed up against the side of the canyon, peddled moonshine liquor to the Sioux, took himself a squaw.' Baxter trickled smoke, said softly, 'Now the man's going home, Adam, with a lot of my hard-earned cash — and short of calling for the US Cavalry I can't see what we can do to stop him, or how we're gonna prise him back out once he gets in.'

3

Ordinarily, Jenny Stone would have left a pan of savoury stew simmering on the iron stove, turned the lamp down low in the comfortable front parlour of the rooming-house and gone upstairs to bed long before midnight.

At no time in the past three months had there been more than one guest for her to concern herself with. In the past six weeks there had been none at all, which meant she was on her own for the evening once Ben planted a whiskery kiss on her cheek then stomped out onto the plankwalk and made his way to the Hangdog.

Haven was a town of two women: in summertime, Jenny and Bonnie Darling got an hour or so of pleasant, female company maybe once or twice a month when Dotty Winston and her two girls drove the buggy the long, dusty trail in from the Lazy J. In winter the icy winds moaning across the plains and the steep, jolting ride up a canyon that would most likely be running with flood water meant that friendship took a back seat to comfort and pure common sense. Each year, for a span of three months, company was so one-sided Jenny and Bonnie needed to look often in the mirror to convince themselves they weren't men.

For Jenny, her books were her release, a musty library of misshapen dreams lined up on an old plank shelf nailed in place by Ben. She no longer taught school — heck, even if the kids could have got in from the outlying ranches there was no cash to pay a teacher, no premises suitable for a classroom — but she had never given up her reading and had even, when Ben was laid up with his broken leg, tried her hand at teaching an adult who was reluctant and even downright rebellious, but had no means of escape.

But tonight she was filled with an

uneasiness that was completely at odds with the boredom that usually had her eyelids dropping after no more than a few pages of *Great Expectations*, and that unrest had been forced upon her by the sight of the black-garbed horseman who had appeared like a phantom through the sweeping curtain of rain.

Strangers were a rare breed in Haven. And, as she peered through the net curtains at this rain-soaked rider with the silver coins glinting in his hat, Jenny felt worry hit her like a gripe in the stomach, and for an instant her breath was tight in her chest.

They were old-timers, those men gathered in the Hangdog. Her Ben was ageing, his eyes were weak, and he was tired. Dan Ford was the law — and a reliable man — but he enforced it with a tarnished badge and a belt from which no holster hung. A man didn't carry guns to control the shifting shadows; no weapons were needed to patrol a deserted street where the only movement or sound was caused by the keening wind rattling loose shutters.

A dark, spare woman with soft skin and intelligent blue eyes, dressed ready for bed with a thin pink gown over her nightdress, Jenny Stone watched the dark stranger dismount in front of the saloon and tie his horse at the rail, saw the wash of yellow lamplight catch the hard planes of his glistening wet face as he pushed in through the doors — and from that moment she was unable to relax.

Each familiar creak of settling timber in the old house was magnified in her ears, and became suspicious; each sough of the angry wind brought her back to the window to twitch the curtain and peer out at the street where pools of lamplight swung erratically across glistening, rain-spattered mud.

But the crack of the shot, when it came, sharp, vicious and unmistakable, caught her unawares by the stove in the warm kitchen. Her head jerked as if struck. Her dark eyes widened in horror. And, as she swung away from the stove, off balance, already striding towards the door, the tin pot slipped from her fingers, clattered to the boards and showered her naked feet with scalding coffee.

It had so little effect, it might have been cold water.

Jenny hit the front door running, cried out in her impatience, dragged it open, ran panting out into the freezing cold night. Her bare feet slapped on the plankwalk. The wind whipped at her flimsy nightdress, the loose cotton gown she had brought with her from back East. Then she was down off the plankwalk and in the street, slipping and sliding in slimy, ankle-deep mud as she floundered recklessly towards the ominous silence of the Hangdog Saloon.

★ ★ ★

Sitting on the chill, shadowy window seat nursing the glowing remains of his

34

cigarette, Wilf Gannon knew darn well that, in a land where survival was each man's prime consideration, the arrival of one lean stranger with eyes like slivers of cold steel and a couple of six-guns lashed to his thighs didn't, of itself, constitute any danger.

But he was wise enough not only to trust his own instincts — honed during a lifetime spent in that same savage, lawless land — but to put considerable store on the reactions of his venerable friends. And the way each one of those seasoned old-timers was hunched over the card table being extra careful not to look outside the pool of light towards the dark, menacing figure draped languidly against the bar told him that the conclusions they had reached matched his own.

This man who had strutted arrogantly into their midst and hooked one spurred boot on the rail and his elbows on the bar was a cold-blooded killer. But what the hell he was doing in a ghost town called Haven, staring cold-eyed and calculating at a bunch of tired old derelicts playing poker for heaps of dead lucifers was entirely beyond Wilf's comprehension.

From the look of abstracted puzzlement on the frowning countenance of the town constable as he peered somewhat myopically at his five greasy cards, fathoming the reasons behind the gunman's unexpected appearance was also giving Dan Ford a fair degree of mental strain.

But that was the kind of tension that went with his job, and Dan accepted it. Hank Travis was also reasonably unfazed by the menacing figure over at the bar — hence the growing pile of lucifers in front of him, Wilf thought with a faint smile — whereas others at the table were clearly getting hot under the collar.

About the time the level of whiskey dropped so low in the bottle it was in danger of evaporating dry — Wilf reckoned it would have been close to one o'clock by then — John Darling's chair creaked like an ungreased axle as he eased his bulk back from the table, snapped his red galluses with his thumbs, wiped sweating palms on his apron and cocked an eye towards the stranger.

'Be locking up in about ten minutes, stranger,' he said bluntly.

'Don't mind me,' the dark gunslinger said in a voice like fine gravel sliding down a metal chute. 'Break open a fresh bottle, I'll take it upstairs.'

'Sorry,' John said, and glanced woodenly across at Ben Stone. 'We don't take guests, but if you're after a bed old Ben here runs the rooming-house across the street.'

Ben sighed, flicked a glance at the stranger then shook his head. 'Just your luck, feller,' he said quietly. 'You picked the one night in the whole damn year every room's taken.'

'Yeah,' the stranger said drily. 'I guessed as much when I saw all them broncs tied up at your rail.'

'I run the livery stable down the

street,' Hank Travis said, absently running thick fingers through his unruly grey hair. 'Maybe the horses you didn't see are in there.' His voice was level, his words doing nothing more than state a simple supposition, offer one explanation for an apparent contradiction. Yet to Wilf Gannon, watching from the shadows, it seemed that when Travis tilted his head to look towards the bar his cool grey eyes — without any change in the intensity of their gaze — held a clear challenge that pinned the gunman back against the heavy wood counter.

Held something else, too, Wilf Gannon reckoned. Recognition, maybe — though from across the room he couldn't be sure.

For an instant it was as if each man in that room was holding his breath so that the only sounds — magnified to an intolerable degree in the sudden, aching tension — were the fierce crackling of the pine logs in the glowing stove and the spasmodic,

38

kettledrum beat of the rain.

'It's your livery stable,' the gunman said at last. 'Why don't you tell me? Are they in there — or is your friend a liar?' Deliberately, he placed his empty glass on the bar and came upright, balanced like a dancer on the balls of his feet.

Imperceptibly, a slow inch at a time, Wilf Gannon eased himself out of his seat and began to limp through the shadows towards the rear of the saloon. As he did so he saw the door of the kitchen open an inch at a time and, in the lamplight beyond, could be seen the tall, elegant figure of Bonnie Darling.

'What the hell started this anyway?' Dan Ford grumbled. His hands were flat on the table, covering his face-down cards. A frown pressed a deep furrow in his brow. He was an intelligent man, and the question was far-reaching, like a net cast wide. Trouble had been building up since the black-garbed stranger crashed through the door. But the reasons for it lay elsewhere, and Dan was looking for enlightenment.

And then, as another fierce gust of wind drew a sharp glance from Dan and drove rain rattling against the window, he said bitterly, 'Why don't you just ride on out while you've still got time? There ain't nothing for men like you in Haven.'

'Men like me,' the gunman repeated in that strange, rasping voice, and he nodded slowly as if reaching a decision. 'Well, in time, maybe I would've,' he said easily, and his grin was as chilling as the winter rain. 'But the fat old man who owns this place, he got a mite unsociable. Two of your friends lied for no damn reason. And now you've opened your big mouth and said something mean enough to stick in my craw — though I guess that's what you're paid to do — and whatever it is you reckon's been started in here is about to get finished.'

'Every one of us is unarmed,' Hank Travis said.

'Friend, this is between me and the town constable.'

'Him too,' Hank said.

'That makes it almost too easy to be fun,' the gunman said. And in one fluid movement he dipped his right hand, lifted it to the whisper of oiled leather and now he was holding a six-gun.

To the accompaniment of muttered oaths and the squeal of chair legs on boards, Ben Stone and John Darling dug in their heels and pushed back out of the line of fire. Hank Travis remained still, his cold eyes riveted on the gunman. Dan Ford grunted softly in surprise, but didn't move. He kept his hands flat on the table, in full view, that frown like a deep crevice above his sharp nose.

He was still frowning when the the gunman pulled the trigger.

In that dim, silent room the detonation was like a charge of dynamite going off, ringing in the ears, the muzzle flash a streak of lightning reflected off the rain-spattered windows and dazzling the eyes.

The slug drilled a neat black hole

through the centre of the tarnished badge pinned to Dan Ford's chest. He went over backwards, crashed heavily to the floor amid the splintered wreckage of his chair.

The last hand of cards he would ever play, dragged with him as his lifeless hands slid off the table, fluttered down onto his chest. The dead matches he had won pattered to the boards.

In a continuation of the fluid movement that started the murderous act, the killer lowered the hammer by allowing the six-gun to tilt back in his palm until the barrel was vertical. Then, in a blur of movement, he spun the pistol forwards, then backwards and down to sock into its holster.

It was that deliberate act of braggadocio that, more than anything, drove Wilf Gannon at a furious, limping run into the Hangdog's kitchen to brush wordlessly past Bonnie Darling into the dark wet alley behind the Hangdog and on around to angle across the muddy street.

His destination was the loft above Hank Travis's livery stable that for six months of the year he called his home.

And all he could see through his cold, blind rage was the dull sheen of the saddle he used as a pillow and, beyond it, the scarred leather scabbard containing his old, battered Henry repeater.

4

'Jenny!'

Wilf Gannon roared the words, heard them whipped away by the blustering wind, saw the scantily clad girl stop, white-faced, alongside the sleek black horse that stood with head drooping and its rump turned to the storm at the Hangdog's hitch rail.

Slipping and sliding in the mud, Wilf floundered along the edge of the plankwalk. When he reached Jenny Stone he saw that she was soaked through and shivering, yet he guessed that the trembling that gripped her slim form was as much from fear as from the bitter cold.

'Girl, what the hell are you doing out here?'

'There was a shot — '

'Ben's OK,' Wilf said tersely. 'If anyone's in danger it's Hank — and

I've a hunch he can handle himself till I get there with my old Henry. Come on, let's get you home.'

He pulled her softness into the curve of his left arm, then placed his right arm under her knees and swept her off her feet. As he turned towards the rooming-house the wind gusted and Wilf swayed like a tree giving under the axe, felt his boots shift precariously in the mud. Then he had regained firm footing and was splashing awkwardly across the street as Jenny Stone buried her face into the hollow of his neck and he was conscious of her musk perfume, felt her warm breath and the hot wetness of tears.

In her haste, Jenny had left the rooming-house door open. It swung to and fro, crashing loosely against the inner wall. The wind drove into the hallway, rippling the thin carpet, dashing the papered walls with rain. Oil lamps danced and flickered eerily.

Grunting, Wilf climbed onto the plankwalk with his burden, rocked sideways to come up with his shoulder against a timber upright — and heard the catch of Jenny's breath as she lifted her head to watch a horseman gallop forth from the open doors of Hank Travis's livery stable.

'Goddamn!' Wilf swore softly.

'Indian,' Jenny whispered.

For the man who had raced across the street on a diagonal course and leapt from his mount on the wrong — the Indian — side, had a mane of raven hair brushing his shoulders and, as he bounded up onto the plankwalk fronting the Hangdog, the watchers saw, in the faint light, that his nose was a proud, fierce hook, his eyes black and glittering above high cheekbones.

★   ★   ★

'Let's ride.'

Moses 'Streak' Kane was already climbing to his feet as he uttered the words, and when Frank Tighe blinked and opened his mouth as if to protest,

46

Kane swung a booted foot in a wild kick that showered the sputtering, smoking fire — and Tighe — with heavy clods of earth and wet leaves.

'For Christ's sake!' Tighe yelled, toppling backwards off his heels onto the seat of his pants and spilling hot coffee into his lap.

'You move when I tell you,' Kane said easily, his lips twitching as he watched the seated man slapping at his scalded thighs.

'Hell fire, Streak,' Dakota Slim drawled, 'I'll bet Frank wishes he could change his pants as fast as you change your mind and your tactics.' He was away from the fire, sheltered and dry under the rocky outcrop, a dark shape pinpointed by the glowing tip of his cigarette. 'What the hell happened to them two hours, anyway?'

'Two hours for a gunslinger like Django Orr to tame a ghost town occupied by a handful of old-timers living on fading dreams?' Kane's laugh was mocking. He walked away from the ruins of the fire, began tightening the big roan's saddle cinch and checking the rawhide bindings securing the two heavy sacks. 'We've given him an hour — and even that's too long for us to set tight in this goddamn rain with a posse breathing down our necks.'

Frank Tighe swore softly as he rose, shook himself down then bent to recover the coffee pot from the smouldering embers. 'I already told you that,' he said, 'so why's it taken you a whole hour to figure out you was wrong in the first place?'

Kane watched Tighe stow away the cooking utensils, reached for the pommel and swung himself atop the roan and said with deceptive mildness, 'You telling me I made a mistake, Frank?'

'Back off, Moses. The man's asking you why the hell you split us up and wasted a whole damn hour with a posse breathing down our necks — then start shoutin' your mouth off as if all the time *we* was in the wrong,' Dakota Slim growled. He emerged from the shelter

48

of the overhang, stretched, spat, and as he moved to his horse in the rustling, dripping darkness his wayward eye was almost luminous.

'If I gave that impression, I apologize,' Kane said drily. 'Now will the both of you for Christ's sake mount up so we can get the hell out of here!'

Tighe was already in the saddle, a blocky shape in a slicker, huddled miserably beneath the low, dripping branches. Dakota Slim's teeth flashed, and as he gathered the reins and swung over leather he said, 'Tell me, Frank, what can you hear?'

'Wind and rain. My own goddamn teeth chattering,' Tighe said.

'I think that's what's bothering old Streak,' Slim said sardonically. 'He's been listenin' to all that noise roaring in his ears and come to the conclusion that while we're out in the open and damn near blind and deaf, that posse could be closin' in.'

'Yeah,' Streak said, grinning savagely, 'but what makes me top man and you *segundo* is that by the time you reached the same conclusion — it'd be too late.'

'Nah,' Slim scoffed as they moved off towards the trail, riding into the wind through a tangle of dark branches that slashed at horses and men. 'It'd been me, we'd've rode in with Orr and Young Fox.'

'And maybe wound up dead,' Streak Kane said, lifting an arm to ward off a whipping branch as he broke through the brush, emerged onto clear, open ground, and reined in.

'My way was right,' he insisted, as the other two men rode alongside, the wind a fierce blast flapping slickers and Stetsons, the rain needle-sharp in its driven intensity. 'But one hour was long enough — maybe too long. If Django Orr's hit trouble we'll meet Young Fox on the way in. But that ain't what's bothering me. Sure, I've been listening to the wind and rain, and with good reason. In weather like this it seems like all the water in the Bighorns comes tumbling down High Falls to flood the dry wash cutting through the canyon to the east of Haven. That mass of tumbling white water gets squeezed tight in Twin Bluffs Pass. If we ride fast and hard, we'll make it before that happens. If we don't, well, the way ahead'll be blocked and that posse'll have at least six clear days to take three sitting ducks and hang 'em high.'

★ ★ ★

Mort Baxter had hit the kind of trouble that frequently besets the leader of a posse made up of ordinary citizens with businesses to run.

Full bellies and the tobacco-scented warmth of a straw-filled loft had induced a comfortable lethargy in which the tired minds of intelligent men were so biased that they inaccurately judged their present situation and saw ahead of them only one sensible course: with the weather worsening, Streak Kane and his men were too far ahead to be caught before they made it through

Twin Bluffs Pass into the canyon stronghold; it was time for the posse to get a night's sleep, then head for home territory and telegraph for professional help.

They'd made that clear to Mort Baxter. He knew their minds were set, beyond changing.

Baxter understood that line of thinking, knew darned well he'd be of the same mind if he didn't have a capable foreman overseeing the day-to-day running of his own ranch, and hadn't lost so much hard cash to the bank robbers that he could see ahead of him at best some three years' hard work to recoup his losses, at worst the bleak misery of financial ruin.

And yet, relaxing in the big main room of Adam Flint's ranch house, boots off, cigarette glowing and a glass of expensive whiskey at his elbow, Baxter was finding that, even for him, those bleak prospects were paling in the face of what lay ahead if he kept up the hunt.

Alone, one middle-aged rancher up against five armed outlaws, all he was likely to do was get himself killed. And he knew that long years of friendship gave him no right to ask for help from Adam Flint.

'This ain't your fight, Adam,' he said now, giving voice to his thoughts. 'I'll rest here overnight, tomorrow you point the way, I'll ride.'

'Twin Bluffs Pass'll be a raging torrent for days,' Flint said bluntly. 'Only other way you *might* get to Haven is to ride north over the rocky high ground, swing in around the top end of the canyon then make your way on foot down through the wooded slopes. As far as I know it ain't ever been done — and in this weather, it'd be asking for trouble.'

He leaned forward out of his deep leather chair, poked pensively at the glowing logs in the big stone grate with a bent old running iron, then sighed heavily.

'What I'm saying, Mort,' he said,

twisting his skinny, corded neck to peer at the stocky rancher, 'is that with all that rain and those goddamn outlaws there ain't no way into that canyon without either breaking your neck on the climb down from the rimrock, or getting drilled full of holes if you do make it in one piece.'

In the shadows by the long table, John Gray, Flint's tall, rawboned foreman cleared his throat. 'But what you ain't sayin', Adam, is that one way or another someone sure as hell has got to get into Haven — and get in there fast.'

Mort Baxter frowned. 'I don't understand.'

Flint sent the running iron clattering into the hearth and unwound out of his chair. He glanced across at Gray as a match flared, then turned to stand with his back to the fire, thumbs hooked in his belt.

'All we've got here's a skeleton crew, Mort. Winter comes, I pay off the hands, hire again in spring.' He paused, his face darkening. 'One of the men I lay off is an old-timer called Wilf Gannon. Must be close to seventy years old. Used to own a ranch, now drives my chuck wagon and works some kind of magic with a hot iron skillet.'

'Lives in Haven,' Gray said, chair creaking as he crossed his long legs, trickled smoke through his nostrils. 'Along with a bunch of maybe five or six old-timers who stayed on when the speculators and prospectors rode out. But, of them all, Wilf Gannon is the one Streak Kane has a mighty special reason for hating.'

'I kinda like that old feller,' Flint said softly, letting a faint smile touch his lips as he caught John Gray's slow nod of agreement. 'Like 'em all, as a matter of fact — so you could say, Mort, that when you lost a posse you gained a couple of fellers with a lot more interest in this than the need to recover some missing banknotes.'

'I could, but I still wouldn't know why all this urgency,' Baxter said bluntly. He watched as Gray rose from his chair and, with easy familiarity, wandered across to the crystal decanter on the big roll-top desk; knew he was seeing here not just a capable foreman, but the man childless bachelor Adam Flint had selected to take over the big spread when he was too old or just too plain tired to continue — and for an instant Mort Baxter felt a warm satisfaction for his friend.

Then, as Gray poured his whiskey and drifted to the window to gaze out at the black, wet night, Baxter, somewhat baffled, knowing he was missing something, said, 'Cut down to the bare bones, all Streak Kane is doing is riding home with a heap of somebody else's cash after fifteen years in the wilderness, Adam. If that should make you fearful for your cook's safety, then I reckon there's trees out there preventing me from seeing some mighty important wood.'

'D'you ever hear what happened to that old miner who put Haven on the map?' Gray asked. He turned away from the window, glass in hand, and Baxter shrugged, jutted his lower lip.

'Only that he got run out of town by a lot of disgruntled miners fed up to the back teeth of digging holes in a barren hillside. Headed south, still with that dream of making a fortune?' He cocked a questioning eyebrow at the big foreman.

Gray nodded. 'Pointed his skinny old mule t'wards New Mexico, planned on doin' some digging in the Sangre de Cristo.' He paused, let the silence build, said, 'A couple of waddies found him hanging from a live oak, his eyes pecked out. He never even made the border.'

'Ah,' Mort Baxter said softly.

'Common knowledge Streak Kane hanged him,' Adam Flint said, lifting his chin as he massaged the back of his neck. 'He blamed that crazy old man for turning Haven into a mining camp, went kind of *loco* himself. That put him in trouble with some of the tougher elements in town, and Kane found it convenient to quit the canyon no more than a week after the old feller had bounced out of town on that bony mule with his eyes wild and the rattle of gunfire ringin' in his ears.'

Mort Baxter nodded slowly. He bent forward, grunted as he hauled on his boots, stood up and stamped a couple of times to settle his feet then knelt and buckled on his spurs. When he stood again the loose-drilled Mexican peso rowels tinkled faintly.

'That's only a part of it, Adam,' John Gray said, absently watching Baxter while his thoughts ranged elsewhere. He moved forward into the circle of lamplight, saw Flint concede the point with a curt nod, tossed back his drink. 'Although Kane's got a seething hatred of one particular old-timer, he blamed every man who rode into Haven, Baxter,' he went on. 'But at that time there were just too many tough *hombres* packing pistols for him to take on all by hisself.'

'But now there ain't,' Mort Baxter

concluded, sudden understanding turning his face bleak. 'From what you've told me he's a vengeful man. Toting a couple of gunny-sacks packed with stolen cash he'll be cock-a-hoop — and right now he's riding into a canyon town that's likely to be sealed off for days, carrying with him ten years' hatred directed at half-a-dozen old-timers who don't even know he's in the same territory.'

'Did that mercantile feller have any other names dancin' a jig on the tip of his tongue?' John Gray asked.

Mort stuck out his lips, breathed deep through flared nostrils. 'One thing led to another,' he admitted. 'Kane was known to ride with a feller called Dakota Slim, made his name up in that Territory before drifting south. A crazy 'breed name of Orr. A full-blood young Sioux wasn't in the bank raid, joined 'em later for some reason. It was after that they headed north.' He shrugged. 'Another man name of Tighe, done time, weak but dangerous . . . '

Adam Flint laughed softly. 'You make it sound real bad, Mort,' he said, moving away from the dying fire to push the whiskey decanter to one side and rummage through the litter of papers on his desk. He came up with a creased sheet scrawled with a network of spidery lines and blotched with faded washes of colour, carried it to the big table and with his calloused palms smoothed it flat.

'Only trouble is,' he said as the two watching men joined him and their long shadows fell across the open map, 'as John will reluctantly confirm, the picture still ain't complete.'

Leaning over the table on stiff arms, his hands either side of the old map he had sketched years back when as a raw newcomer he had first been led through the rugged Bighorn Country, Adam Flint said, 'Streak Kane ain't just a vengeful man, Mort, he's a lustful womanizer. John Darling owns the general store, and the Hangdog Saloon. His wife Bonnie's a fine woman, but maybe too old to interest Kane.' He shook his head sorrowfully. 'But up in Haven there's also a pretty young schoolmarm name of Jenny Stone — wife of another of those old-timers — whose sensible skirts are likely to give a certain kind of man — more so now he's drunk with power and success — all the wrong ideas.'

5

The wind moaned across the open doorway of Hank Travis's livery stable as Wilf Gannon made his way down its wide runway. The office where Hank bunked was in darkness. One of the half-dozen horses in the stalls on either side of the runway nickered softly. Timber creaked as another leaned its weight against a thin partition. Loose straw rustled to the wind's fierce flurries, flying strands borne on the draughts scratching Gannon's face as he hurried past the stalls to where the ladder rose towards the high loft.

As he climbed the shaky framework he thought briefly of Jenny Stone, hoped she had enough sense to follow his directions and lock and bar the rooming-house's back and front doors. Then, exertion causing him to breathe hard in the darkness, old Wilf allowed himself a mirthless grin.

Barred doors wouldn't stop a man like that black-hearted killer — and there never had been any way of stopping an Indian bent on mischief.

But there was only two of them, Wilf reminded himself, as he stepped up onto the uneven floor of the loft and stumbled through the gloom to the corner formed by the back and side walls which, with straw bales and a couple of draped horse blankets, was for six months of the year transformed into a cosy room that was warm, draught-free and just about as private as a man could wish for.

Then he was down on his knees, pulling aside cardboard boxes of possessions, bumping and rattling the old hanging lantern with the crown of his hat, bending low to fumble behind the McClellan saddle that doubled as a pillow for the supple scabbard — and his Henry repeater.

'Just two of 'em,' he said again, softly, scornfully, settling back on his heels and running his hands along the cold gleam of the metal barrel, the smooth, worn stock, 'and neither one of 'em saw me, so neither one of 'em's likely to expect a man with a gun to come a-walkin' boldly through that saloon door to blast 'em to Hell and gone!'

The oiled rattle of the rifle's action as Wilf jacked a shell into the breech was shockingly loud in the muffled quiet of the loft, and for an instant his old ears were dead to other sounds.

Then his head jerked around as, from the windswept street there came the muted beat of hooves muffled by mud. With a muttered curse, Wilf scrambled across the rough, straw covered boards to the livery stable's front wall.

Down on one knee, Wilf swept off his Stetson and pressed his forehead to the wall, squinting through a wide chink between the boards, blinking to clear his vision as the icy draught flooded his eyes with stinging tears.

He grunted in dismay.

Through the rain swept mud that

glistened shiftingly in the sweeping yellow light from the rooming-house's wildly swinging lantern, three men in shiny slickers rode up the hill and wheeled their horses towards the Hangdog's hitch rail. The butts of saddle guns jutted from beneath lean thighs. As they swung down and tethered their horses, slickers were swept back to expose pistols in tied-down holsters.

One man paused long enough in the driving rain to remove two heavy gunny-sacks that were slung behind his saddle.

Then they were up on the plankwalk, and Wilf Gannon blinked in disbelief as, for the second time that night — Christ, for the second time in as long as he could remember! — the door of the Hangdog Saloon was kicked open.

It swung to behind the gunmen. Faintly, to Wilf Gannon's ears, there came the creak of its hinges, the slap of wood on wood.

And as he listened absently to those

mournful sounds, he was seeing again through eyes blinded by cold tears the powerful figure swinging down from the big roan gelding and slinging the bulging gunny-sacks over his shoulder, seeing the greying hair tied back — Indian fashion — with a rawhide thong, and raking the dying embers of his memory for a long-forgotten name . . .

* * *

Inside the Hangdog Saloon the silence was unnerving.

The young Indian slipped in through the doors ahead of a flurry of cold air, swept an all-seeing glance across the men grouped around the table and the black-clad gunman sitting with out-stretched legs in a straight-backed chair up against the bar, then without a word began to prowl the big room on feet cushioned by soft elk-hide moccasins. He seemed to drift in and out of the deepest shadows, the weak lamplight now catching the glistening sleekness of his wet, raven hair, now winking like bright sparks in the man's liquid black eyes.

As he circled the room, the three tired, grey men sitting at the table remained unnaturally still, their only sign of life the first swift exchange of glances at this fresh development, the slight turn of a head as one or the other strained to keep the prowling Indian in view; the subtle, momentary change in their demeanour almost undetectable, but there nonetheless, whenever their watchful eyes happened across the still, bloody figure that had so recently been their friend, Dan Ford.

Then the Indian was back in the circle of light, there almost without their hearing or noticing, and the chair creaked as the gunman crossed his long legs and said softly, 'You reckon it's safe for us to breathe, now, Young Fox?'

'Maybe.' The Indian was no more than nineteen, of medium height but lithe and sinewy with sloping shoulders and the lazy movements of a stalking wildcat. Bright, intelligent eyes were deep set beneath a bony brow. High cheekbones cast shadows leading to a mobile mouth bracketed by lines that suggested a lot of laughter. But it showed no signs of humour now as he said, 'You killed one, Django, got three look scared half to death but could be fooling.' He hooked a chair with his foot, straddled it, grinned suddenly. 'But there's someone else in here you ain't seen yet — and already one man's got away.'

The gunman's eyebrows lifted. The jut of his lips was mocking. 'You're dreaming, Young Fox. You're a redskin living so far in the past you're seeing spirits, dreaming up tracks in a saloon-bar's dust. There ain't nobody in here, ain't nobody lef — '

'Ask them!'

The words cut like the crack of a whip. Over at the table John Darling cleared his throat. 'There's nobody else, not in here,' he said quietly. 'My wife's

68

in back of the mercantile next door. If you want to check you can get there through the kitchen — but she's in bed asleep.'

'All right,' said the Indian called Young Fox, nodding his satisfaction. 'Not here, but close enough. So what about the one that got away?'

Darling shrugged. 'I don't know what you're talking about.'

'What I'm talking about,' Young Fox said, 'is the man who smoked a cigarette over by the window, left a sack of Bull Durham on the table, maybe left by the back door when the great Django Orr was playing with his beeg peestol.'

The lean gunman came smoothly up out of the chair, glanced across at the slack pouch trailing shreds of tobacco across the window table, then walked away from the bar towards the three oldtimers and snorted dismissively, 'Young Fox, that big pistol took care of Haven's lawman just like Streak wanted,' he said in clipped, angry tones. 'He sent me in because he never did put no faith in a goddamn Indian armed with a pig-sticker — and in between the time I walked through that door and plugged the old-timer with the badge, there ain't *nobody* snuck out of here.'

The Indian shrugged. 'The man who'd know most about that,' he said placidly, 'is the man who was holed up in the livery stable with his pig-sticker, watching your back.'

'Or these three old-timers,' said Django Orr, jerking his thumb at the occupants of the table, 'and from them you already got your answer.'

'They lied,' Young Fox said bluntly.

Again John Darling spoke up. 'Is this important?' he asked. He looked questioningly at Django Orr on one side of the table, then across at the Indian. 'I told you no deliberate lie, only what I know: there was four of us here, now there's three of us left alive. We'd played cards all night. If there was another man over there, well, he sure escaped my notice.'

'And Orr's,' Young Fox commented drily. 'Big man, walked down the alley out of here, was in time to grab hold of a half naked woman, carry her back across the street.'

'Jesus!' Ben Stone breathed, the light glinting on his spectacles as he turned to look at the Indian.

'What it is, you got a beeg peestol, Django,' Young Fox said, 'but you ain't got no brains.' And as the gunman hissed through clenched teeth and swung towards him, right hand hovering relaxed and ready over his jutting six-gun, the Indian's chair went clattering across the room and with a smooth fluid movement that was almost lazy in its execution, he was up on his feet and waiting and, held by the broad blade, a big knife glittered in his sinewy hand.

They were standing like that, poised, one man's face suffused with hatred, the other's showing nothing but the eternal patience of his race, when again the doors of the Hangdog Saloon

71

crashed open and the winds of winter gusted in presaging the entry of three yellow-slickered gunmen.

'Enough!' Streak Kane roared, and suddenly all was silent and still.

Slicker swept back, gunny-sacks hanging heavy from his left shoulder and right hand brushing his holster, Kane let his eyes rake the room. His sweeping glance delved into the gloomy corners, returned to take in the three unarmed old-timers sitting tense around the table, the stiffening, lifeless figure of Dan Ford; the two, poised antagonists.

Then he laughed softly. His hand left his holster to dash rain water from his face. The sound of the gunny-sacks thumping to the boards broke the spell.

Dripping water, Frank Tighe stomped past him, went round the end of the bar and grabbed a bottle off the shelf, pulled the cork with his teeth. Dakota Slim walked over to the dead town constable, gazed down at the sightless eyes, touched the tarnished badge with the toe of his boot.

Slowly, flexing stiff fingers, Django Orr backed off. Young Fox, the Indian, made no apparent movement, yet the knife was gone from his hand and now jutted from its fringed scabbard.

'John Darling, Ben Stone,' Streak Kane said, studying faces. 'Ten years older but no damn wiser or you'd both be long gone from this godforsaken canyon.' He paused, then said softly, 'And you, Hank Travis.'

His voice changed on the last name, became brittle yet thoughtful, and he glanced across at Django Orr as if expecting a reaction. But, his brief stand-off with the Indian over and done with, the gunman had joined Frank Tighe at the bar, and was already taking a deep pull from the bottle.

'I still don't know what this is all about,' Travis said carefully, 'but what I see I don't like. What the hell kind of lawlessness brings you back here, Moses Kane?'

'He don't like it, Streak,' Dakota Slim said mockingly. 'He thinks maybe we're operating on the wrong side of the law.' And he bent down, removed the tarnished badge from Dan Ford's chest and, with deliberation, pinned it on his own shirt-front.

'That takes care of that,' Kane said. 'What about your end, Django?'

The gunman dragged the back of his hand across his mouth, coughed the fumes out of his throat, said raspingly, 'Ghost town was a pretty good guess, Streak. Only people left in Haven are these three unarmed fellers and a woman who runs the boarding house with one of them.' He shrugged, flicked a venomous glance at the Indian. 'There's maybe one more around somewheres, but over that there's some dispute.'

Kane's eyebrow lifted in mock surprise. 'Between you two?' He looked at Young Fox, and the Indian sneered.

'There's no dispute. I came over from the livery when I heard the shot. Just about then a big feller came out of the alley, spoke to a dark-haired young woman wearing nothing but thin nightclothes out there in the storm. He picked her up and carried her back across the street.'

A soft sigh escaped from Ben Stone's lips. Behind the spectacles his eyes closed.

Streak Kane walked over to the bar, took the bottle off Frank Tighe, drank deeply. Then he sighed, wiped the neck of the bottle with his hand, turned back to the room.

'The town's changed,' he said. 'I don't know of no rooming-house, but if there is one, and a woman runs it, that must've been her you saw, Young Fox.' He looked at Darling, said, 'John, this is your place, has been ever since that old Forty-niner raised a thirst shouting his mouth off about gold and you set about making some for yourself.' He turned his gaze on Hank Travis. 'I reckon for you to get tied up with a gal, or any business that don't involve horses or guns, is plumb out of character. My guess is you run the livery stable.' He raised an eyebrow, got a nod of admission in return. His eyes finally settled on Ben Stone. 'That makes her your woman, feller.'

'You're doin' the talking.'

'So what happened, d'you get lucky, or what?'

Stone frowned. 'Ask Dan Ford. If he could talk, he'd tell you any luck any of us had sneaked out the door when your gunman walked in.'

Kane laughed, tossed the bottle to Tighe. 'You've got all the luck you can handle,' he said, 'if you can get a purty young woman to care for you at your time of life.' He paused, watching. 'So, what did she want over here?'

Ben Stone drew a deep breath, let it out slowly. 'She heard a shot. Maybe she was worried.' He shrugged.

Kane widened his eyes in mock surprise. 'Must've been some worried to come running out in the street with no clothes on,' he said, then pursed his lips. 'Or maybe that wasn't it. Maybe she came out to meet that other feller we ain't seen yet.'

Stone smiled a twisted smile, and shook his head. 'No.'

A match flared. Dakota Slim lifted his cupped hands, applied flame to his cigarette. He blew smoke, squinted through it at Moses Kane. 'Whether or not she intended to,' he said, 'if we believe Young Fox she's surely ended up in his arms — so maybe we'd best get on over there.'

'If a big feller took that gal in off the street, he'll most likely use a shotgun to keep us at bay,' Moses Kane said with what seemed like relish, and now there was a stirring within him, a wildness pulsating just beneath the surface. 'There's a pattern here, Slim. I see these three fellers, I expect to see a fourth. Hell, even ten years back you saw one, you'd just know the others'd be close by.' He looked at the three men at the table, fixed his eyes on each in turn then let his gaze become unfocused as he said softly, 'That other man is Wilf Gannon — and if I had to have a reason for returning to Haven, it'd be that meddling bastard that'd draw me back here like iron filings to a magnet.'

'All right,' said Dakota Slim. 'But on a a night like this him and the girl could be just about anywhere — '

'Gannon's an old man, but that don't take away his toughness,' Moses Kane snapped. 'If he's out there, he's dangerous, and I'd advise every one of you from now on to tread careful.' The dark eyes glittered as he took a deep breath. 'But Wilf Gannon'll keep. First, we figure out what to do with these three fellers.'

'Django Orr didn't wait to do no thinking, which surely took care of Dan Ford,' Hank Travis said. 'You got similar ideas, Kane?'

'It'd make things easier,' Kane admitted, moving away from the bar, 'and maybe hasten the inevitable.'

'Just say the word,' Django Orr said, and the Indian hissed softly through his teeth and moved towards the door, opened it and held it against the solid pressure of the moaning wind. Rain spattered his moccasins, soaked darkly into the board floor.

'John, if I remember right you had yourself a wife, name of Bonnie,' Kane said, raising his voice and looking at Darling. 'She still around?'

'Out back,' Django Orr said, and grinned towards the doors. 'Young Fox saw her in one of his Injun dreams.'

Ignoring him, Kane went on, 'Go join her, John, keep her warm. But listen: you get it into your head to be a hero, your wife'll be the first to die. You understand that?'

John Darling's laugh was bitter as he rose heavily from his chair. 'Bonnie was kinda fond of Dan Ford,' he said as, with a gait made awkward by stiffness, he headed towards the kitchen. 'She'll be right happy to renew your acquaintance.'

'So that's him took care of,' Kane said dismissively as the door slammed. 'Which leaves Travis and Stone — so maybe now's the time to head on over the street.'

Frank Tighe set the empty bottle on the bar, said carefully, 'Goin' in blind against a man holed up with a shotgun don't make a lot of sense.'

'Yeah, but those two'll be leadin' the way,' Kane said cheerfully. Then, turning, 'Young Fox, you reckon you can get around back of that place without being seen?' but already the words were falling on emptiness. The unattended door where the Indian had been standing swung to and fro in the wind as he melted away into the darkness.

'All right,' Moses Kane said, and the yellow slicker rustled as, almost absently, he drew his six-gun and thumbed back the hammer. 'You two,' he told Stone and Travis, 'climb out of those chairs and lead the way across the street. If you've got any ideas about dropping flat in the mud so your mysterious friend can use that shotgun — forget it. Three of us'll be right behind you. You go down, you won't ever get up.

'Frank, you bring those sacks.'

Ben Stone led the way, closely followed by Travis. The wind hit them as they left the shelter of the Hangdog. The two men leaned into it, their boots kicking up a spray of thin mud as they stepped down into the street. Then they were splashing across towards the rooming-house, light glistening on their wet shoulders as they entered the shifting yellow pool cast by the swinging lantern.

As they stepped up onto the plank-walk in front of the rooming-house, the front door swung open, then back.

Ben Stone took a step forward, held the door wide with his left boot; peered down the hallway, called softly, 'Wilf? You in there?'

'Go on in!' Moses Kane roared.

Hank Travis glanced over his shoulder, spat in disgust. The three gunmen were almost lost in the shadows between the Hangdog's door and its wide window, dim backlight glinting on the drawn guns.

81

' 'Three of us'll be right behind you',' Travis repeated sardonically.

'Yeah,' Ben Stone said, reaching up to wipe his spectacles. 'One hell of a long way behind.'

'So why don't we walk in, walk straight out the back door?'

'Because maybe Young Fox, the Injun'll have other plans for us.'

Travis grunted. 'Don't you keep an old Remington stashed away somewheres?'

'Kitchen,' Ben Stone said, and stepped into the hall.

And, somewhere in front of them, a pistol was noisily cocked. A shadow moved, became a broad-shouldered figure with lank dark hair and a grin that exposed flashing white teeth.

'Young Fox,' Hank Travis said bitterly, as the Indian padded forwards. 'I guess he found your pistol.'

'But not a lot more,' the Indian said. 'The woman was here — but I guess she left in a hurry because all I can find is a wet nightdress.'

82

6

In the hours before dawn the wind dropped but the rain persisted as a steady downpour that drummed on the roofs, cascading through the ripped tarpaper walls of the town's ruined shacks and turning the street into a wide, slow-moving swamp.

Fifty yards behind the livery stable, the ground on which Haven was built — sloping steeply up towards the northern heights but reasonably level east to west — turned rocky then fell away sharply into a deep draw that was a canyon within a canyon. Here the swollen waters tumbled in a raging brown flood, roaring downhill towards the narrow gap of Twin Bluffs Pass.

Moses Kane judged shrewdly that neither Ben Stone nor Hank Travis, numb with weariness and shock, was likely to slip away on such a night. So, having directed them towards rooms on the upper floor of the house that had previously been searched for weapons, he and his two henchmen spread their bedrolls downstairs in the parlour and settled down for what was left of the night.

Kane slept with his head resting on the two stuffed gunny-sacks.

Of his own volition, and to Django Orr's amused contempt, Young Fox went out into the storm and took all five horses down to the livery stable, led them into vacant stalls and made sure they had feed.

The other men were already asleep when he returned. He unrolled his blankets at the foot of the stairs, and slept with his hand on his knife.

* * *

Earlier that same evening, Wilf Gannon had peered out through the Hangdog's rain-streaked windows and told himself that only fools or villains would be abroad on such a night.

In most respects he was right.

But there were other people inhabiting the wooded hills and lush grasslands close to High Falls Canyon who viewed the approach of each cruel winter not with dread, but with a stoicism born out of a religious belief that the land they lived on was borrowed for each man's lifetime, and that the most powerful forces of nature could never be changed.

It was these people who had been pushed back remorselessly by the white man's coming, had watched with hatred as the vast herds of buffalo were massacred by men blazing away indiscriminately with their powerful long rifles for financial gain — or for nothing more rewarding than the sheer, primitive excitement of the kill.

And the helpless onlookers had gazed over the limitless plains littered with rotting carcasses and realized, with anger and bewilderment, that their age-old beliefs were being challenged.

It was these people, too, who had experienced a thousand personal and tribal tragedies as the invaders craftily gained their confidence by lying and cheating, plied the chiefs and warriors with cheap rotgut whiskey to addle their brains then demanded that they make their mark on worthless pieces of paper — masquerading under the grand title of 'treaties' — that offered them justice while taking away their homelands.

One Indian who viewed the white man with mixed feelings was Long Arrow, a Sioux brave from the fertile Powder River country who, in a long ago spring, had returned to his tribe from a solitary deer hunt to discover that, while washing clothes at the creek, his only daughter had been taken to a shack in High Falls Canyon by a man called Moses Kane. No rescue was possible. News of a gold strike had spread, and the canyon was alive with men pouring in through Twin Bluffs Pass, staking claims and digging on the steep, wooded slopes.

The daughter's name was Smooth Skin. She was gone for twelve long months during which Long Arrow and his wife, Pleasant Ways, had remained with their tribe while proudly fighting to hide their grief.

Then, in the same month of the following spring, to the shrill, excited cries of their four-year-old son, Smooth Skin, their daughter, unexpectedly walked into their lodge. Gaunt, eyes haunted with shame and dark with weariness, she had been returned to them by another white man.

This man's name was Wilf Gannon.

But that had been more than fifteen years ago. Since then the Sioux brave called Long Arrow had mellowed and grown old beyond his years as he watched the great chief Red Cloud finally agree to peace, had learned with deep sorrow of the slaughter of Black Kettle's band at the Washita and, in a rare and precious moment, celebrated the death of Custer — the legendary

Yellowhair — at the battle of the Little Bighorn.

News of Sitting Bull's imprisonment was met with disbelief; Chief Joseph's dramatic race for freedom with the Nez Perce had been followed with pride. Now, in direct contravention of the government's laws, Long Arrow was leaving the reservation to make his own personal break for freedom, taking his wife and daughter south in a battered old chuck wagon with an often ripped canvas cover that, this black and windy night, was letting in more cold rain than it kept out.

As he lay awake in his blankets listening to the drip of water and the soughing of the breeze, Long Arrow came to a decision: when he eased the wagon down from the Bighorn foot-hills, and before he made the long drive south to the sun, he would make one last call on his old friend, Adam Flint.

It was a decision that was to alter the course of events, and shift the balance of power in and around the Hangdog Saloon.

* * *

In the warm ranch house many miles to the south of Haven, Adam Flint, Mort Baxter and John Gray talked into the early hours. The rich aroma of fine whiskey was heavy on air already thick with the smoke from cigarettes and cigars, the atmosphere seemingly relaxed and congenial. But, in the long silences, the tired eyes of all three men had assumed the peculiar blankness of withdrawal into self that comes with the awareness of trouble, the knowledge that circumstances were such that unless they acted decisively, and fast, good men would die.

The motives forcing each man to seek the solution to an apparent impasse were vastly different, yet utterly compelling.

Mort Baxter was a businessman facing ruin. Adam Flint was a humane rancher who had fought a war that imbued in him a deep hatred of violence, yet who now believed that an older man — a summer-time employee who was also a close friend — was faced with a threat that would come at him from the darkness with the unexpectedness and speed of a striking cougar.

John Gray listened, drank his share of whiskey and in his deep Texan drawl spoke mostly to agree with the suggestions of the older men. Of his own motives relating to the impending violence in Haven he said nothing, yet both Flint and Baxter sensed in the lean foreman an urgency that matched their own. With the wisdom of experience they left it at that. They had a tough, determined ally. They knew full well that the reasons for Gray's participation in whatever transpired would be revealed to them when the man saw fit.

Yet when the wind ceased its moaning, beaten into submission by the drumming downpour, between the three of them they had not come up with any answer to the dilemma other than the obvious one: the only way into Haven was down the treacherous upper slopes of the canyon.

Which meant, in effect, that there *was* no way in. The old-timers, and the women, were on their own.

7

'Somehow,' Wilf Gannon said quietly, 'I've got to get you out of here.'

The light of a steel-grey dawn was filtering through the cracks in the loft's timbers, creeping across the straw to touch the wan face of Jenny Stone.

As soon as they had scrambled up the ladder Gannon had given her his blanket, watched her wrap herself into a tight cocoon, waited anxiously for the spasms of uncontrollable shivering to ease. Despite the warm clothes she had slipped on before they escaped through the rooming-house's back door to dash along the alley to the rear of the livery stable, Gannon was deeply concerned that her earlier foolishness might bring on a serious chill.

For his own comfort he had burrowed into mounds of loose straw, dragging his old Henry with him, eventually feeling the cold on just the tip of his exposed nose. But, although warm, he had slept little during the few hours before dawn. Always he was conscious of the girl's uneasy movements as she dozed fitfully; and the knowledge that sooner or later Moses Kane would organize a systematic search that was unlikely to miss the gloomy loft kept his nerves vibrating like taut banjo strings.

'That's Ben's job, Wilf,' the girl said now. 'I'm his wife, he'll look after me. Besides, if I leave here, I want him with me.' She was sitting with her back to a bale of straw, the blanket draped around her shoulders. Wilf looked at the way the pale light high-lighted her rich dark hair, tried to forget how long it was since he had woken with a woman alongside him . . .

'We're talking about the impossible, either way,' he said, loath to raise her hopes. 'Moses Kane'll have those fellers watched so it'll be difficult for any of 'em to slip away. And as far as us gettin' out of here, well, I guess you know what the pass is like after heavy rain.'

'Nevertheless,' she said, forcing a brave smile as she seemed to read his thoughts, 'we can't stay here. Moses Kane left Haven months before I arrived with bright eyes and ambitions, but since then enough people have told me about his nature to make me fearful.'

'Yeah,' Wilf said ruefully, 'and I guess I plead guilty. It's too easy to paint lurid pictures about a vicious killer when he's a thousand miles away, just as easy to wish you hadn't when the bastard rides in out of the night — if you'll pardon my language, Jenny.'

She nodded, said softly, 'If it helps, go ahead. A man like you has memories, Wilf, good ones and bad. If half of what Ben told me about you is true, I couldn't be with a better man.'

Wilf chuckled. 'Maybe both of us exaggerated. Moses Kane may have mellowed with age. I sure ain't as tough as Ben makes out.'

'Why is Kane here? Why are any of them here?'

'Something bad,' Wilf said. 'My guess is they plan on holing up for the winter, sent that black devil and his Injun friend in ahead of them to soften us up.' He stood up favouring an aching hip, said angrily, 'Well, they sure as hell got rid of Haven's only law in a hurry — but what they won't realize is that by shooting down Dan Ford in cold blood they've maybe woken up some rusty old-timers who've been too bored for too damn long.'

'The scent of battle, Wilf?' Jenny Stone asked quietly, and Wilf caught a look on her face that suddenly made him feel ten years younger.

'We ain't likely to get outside help,' he said. 'My guess is we'll be safe here most of the morning. John Darling or Bonnie'll dish up breakfast over at the Hangdog. That'll take some time. Then one of 'em'll point out that Dan needs a proper burial. The cemetery's maybe a mile upslope, tucked in off the trail beyond Kane's old place. He'll be curious to see what's left of it. While they're up there . . . '

Jenny Stone shivered.

Then she looked intently at the grizzled old-timer, saw the honest, time-worn face under its thatch of white hair, saw the look in his faded blue eyes and the strength in his hands as he reached down into the straw for his Henry, and with a sigh she closed her eyes and settled back to wait.

8

The floorboards creaked when Ben Stone, fully clothed, rolled off the bed. He shot a glance towards the open door, held his breath while he listened. Then, hearing nothing but the steady dripping of water and the distant murmur of the swollen creek, he let it go in a measured exhalation and silently padded across the room.

Hank Travis was by the window scrubbing a hand across the misted panes when Stone eased into his room. He scowled, then put a cautionary finger to his lips.

'Still sleeping,' he murmured, jerking a thumb downwards. 'Let's keep it like that.'

'The Injun's stretched out across the stairs,' Ben said. 'Saw the light glint in his eyes. We ain't gettin' out that way.'

Travis grunted. 'You take note of

Moses Kane when he bust into the Hangdog, then later when he followed us across the street?' He saw Stone's puzzled look, said, 'The big feller had two gunny-sacks, never let 'em out of his sight. Heavy ones. So tell me, what would hellions like these be toting, in gunny sacks, on just about the filthiest damn night of the year?'

'Yeah,' Stone said,nodding slowly. 'A man don't need brains to work out those fellers hit something big like a train, or a bank, and are on the run.' He dug the makings out of his shirt, straddled a chair and began working on a cigarette. 'Which means,' he finished, 'if we ain't careful we'll all end up like Dan.'

Hank Travis's face was sober. 'Will anyway,' he said bluntly. 'Way I see it, Moses Kane came back for two reasons: he wants a safe hideout for the winter — and he wants to get even with the men he believes drove him out of Haven.'

Stone applied a match to his

cigarette, thoughtfully shook out the flame. 'That reasoning brings us straight to Wilf Gannon,' he said. 'For what he did, Kane hates Wilf the most of all.'

Travis's eyes crinkled at mention of Gannon. 'Tough old nut,' he said approvingly, and Ben Stone nodded agreement.

'The way he acted last night needed quick thinking, and a whole lot of guts,' he said, and his face hardened, his eyes distant with distasteful memories. 'I don't want Jenny anywhere near the womanizer. The further Wilf's took her, the better I'll like it.'

Travis shook his head. 'Wilf brought her over here, Jenny got dressed, and all of that would have took time. I reckon there's only one place they could be, Ben, and that's too close for comfort.'

For several long minutes both men were silent, busy with their thoughts, their ears attuned to the sounds of men stirring downstairs. Finally, Ben Stone sighed deeply, said, 'So, what have we got going for us, Hank?'

Travis chewed his lip, said quietly, 'John's got a gun-belt over't his place, maybe a couple more rifles. Wilf's old Henry's up in the loft — and I've got me a feeling once he's got Jenny tucked away somewhere reasonably safe he'll be thinking about those guns at the mercantile. But to get his hands on them he'll need Kane and his cronies well out of the way, and that's where Dan Ford comes in.'

Stone smiled grimly. 'Dead, but still doing his best for us. A dead man needs respect, a decent burial. If we're going to bury Dan, we need horses. Horses're in the livery — and so's your guns.'

'One step at a time, Ben,' Travis cautioned. And as a voice roared beneath them and footsteps hammered on the stairs he said, 'And the first step's breakfast, over which we do some talkin' that not only makes good sense, but leads Streak Kane where we want him.'

★　★　★

The big iron stove in the rooming-house was black and cold, the tin pot lying in a mess of dried coffee grounds where Jenny had dropped it.

Moses Kane took one look at the chill room, spat disgustedly at the dark stain where coffee had seeped into the boards, then told Frank Tighe to head over to the Hangdog and get John Darling's wife out of bed and rustling up enough food for eight men.

Ten minutes later, with Ben Stone and Hank Travis in the centre of a heavily armed escort made up of Young Fox, the Indian, Django Orr and Dakota Slim, Kane led the way out of the rooming-house into the chill air of a morning made dismal by a heavy white mist hanging the length and breadth of the wide canyon, and they ploughed across the muddy street to the saloon.

Mindful of the fact that Wilf Gannon had spirited Jenny Stone away from the rooming-house, and was still on the loose, Kane had the heavy gunny-sacks slung from his shoulder.

The Hangdog's door creaked open on complaining hinges. They entered the large room where already the smell of frying beef and eggs was drifting through from the kitchen to hang almost mockingly over the body of a man who had eaten his last meal more than twelve hours in the past.

Travis and Stone ignored the stiffened figure of their friend, but exchanged glances as they went to a table and sat down, Stone to roll a smoke, Travis to fish out one of his foul-smelling cheroots while awaiting their breakfast. The three gunmen — Orr, Slim and Frank Tighe — sat together, mean-eyed and surly, the dark-clad man pointedly slamming his six-gun on the table alongside his concho-studded hat and throwing a murderous warning look towards the two prisoners.

Young Fox, the Indian, drifted away into the shadows where his dark eyes were glittering points of light in an impassive countenance.

Streak Kane crossed the floor and

barged aggressively through the door leading into the kitchen. The murmur of voices, rising in anger, was followed by a the rattle of pans, and minutes later John Darling came through with a grim, sweating face and his arms laden with steaming plates of beef and eggs.

Breakfast was wolfed down by the ravenous outlaws who for a week had been eating snatched meals of tinned sardines or cold jerky.

Hank Travis and Ben Stone ate at a slower pace, their inward looking eyes and the measured working of their jaws indicating the ponderous movement of urgent thoughts that were being directed along once familiar pathways now discovered to be almost impassable through years of disuse.

Both men had grown up in the days when quick wits and a practised facility with handguns kept a man alive. But age and the debilitating effect of a town that was slowly but surely dying around them had blunted their thinking, and their reactions — and there was no clearer proof of that frailty than the body of their friend surrounded by the fallen cards of his last hand of poker.

In the grimmest of ironies, the card lying closest to the bullet hole in Dan Ford's chest was the Ace of Spades.

The clatter of knives and forks on tin plates eventually ceased. A chair creaked as a man relaxed at a table. A match flared, a cigarette was lit, and Dakota Slim's satisfied sigh sent a cloud of smoke rising to be caught and plucked away by the draught.

'A man needs burying,' Hank Travis said into the quiet, then looked up and turned his head to wink covertly as John Darling came out of the kitchen to watch in silence.

'Before that, another needs finding,' Moses Kane said. 'A friend of yours.'

'If he exists, he'll wait,' Travis pointed out.

'The dead man sure ain't going nowhere,' Django Orr gritted, white teeth clamped on a thin black cheroot.

'Only as far as the cemetery. A dead

man lying around ain't healthy,' Ben Stone said. He directed the words at Streak Kane and added, 'Besides, the cemetery's just a little ways past the big house set up against the hillside,' and saw the sudden kindling of awareness in the big, grey-haired outlaw's eyes.

Travis chuckled, taking his cue. 'Was a house,' he reminisced, 'in the old days. Now ain't much more than a falling down pile of rotting timber.'

Kane swore softly, angrily pushed his plate away and rose from the table. 'You two fellers got horses?'

'Across at the livery,' Hank Travis said, and sensed Ben Stone's sudden stillness.

'Three fellers,' Dakota Slim corrected. 'If we go grave digging, John Darling goes with us.'

'And his woman,' Django Orr said. 'Otherwise there'll be another one on the loose, and this one'll make sure she's got a gun.'

'Unless I stay behind, keep her company,' Young Fox said from the shadows, and laughed softly.

'Yeah,' Orr said scornfully. 'And while you're playin' wet nurse, see if you can locate the woman belongs to that nightdress.'

'If I go, my wife goes,' John Darling said, his voice tight. He moved away from the kitchen door, a big balding man without weapons of any kind, his wide belt holding up his belly and a look of cold fury in his eyes.

'I think you've got this all wrong,' Django Orr said. 'You don't tell us: we tell you.' He poked a finger on the table alongside the muzzle of his six-gun, spun it in a half-circle then slapped his palm on the butt. The muzzle pointed at John Darling's belt buckle. With the gun still flat on the table, Orr hooked his finger around the trigger, thumbed back the hammer and grinned.

'Leave it,' Moses Kane said. He swung around, kicked Ben Stone's outstretched foot and said, 'Up on your feet. Every damn one of us'll head up the hill, get this buryin' over with.

You,' — he jabbed a finger at John Darling — 'come with us, your wife stays.' Then turning to his own men, he issued his orders. 'Go with them. Bring my horse, and one for the dead feller. Travis owns those stables, most likely lives over there. Make sure he keeps to the runway, the stalls, don't get a chance to pick up any weapons.'

'I'll get my coat,' Darling said.

'Make sure that's all you get,' Streak Kane said. Then, as the others clattered towards the doors he swung on them and said, 'I ain't heard anybody say much about the feller that's out there somewheres, holded up in one of those shacks, maybe watchin' us right now from the high timber. So hear this: I warned you once, now I'm telling you again: you want to stay alive, watch your backs. Now, move.'

* * *

'Stay quiet,' Wilf Gannon ordered.

In the dimmest corner of the loft,

Jenny Stone shrank back into the deep shadows. Gannon moved ponderously across the boards to the far side of the opening at the top of the ladder, positioned himself so that he could see down without being seen. The Henry was clutched in his big fist. At the first sign of movement he had jacked a shell into the breech.

He had been watching the Hangdog through the chinks in the front wall, had seen the men emerge into the thinning mist to step down into the street. His face had twisted with emotion as he saw Ben Stone and Hank Travis leading the way, had hardened as they were swiftly followed by the two gunmen and the cat-like figure of the Indian, and he had sworn softly as the man with the silver conchos in his hat stiff-armed Ben Stone in the small of the back so that he staggered and almost went down in the glistening mud.

Then Wilf's eyes had returned eagerly to the still swinging doors for a clear daylight sighting of Moses Kane. But the big man with the snatched-back grey hair had not emerged, nor had John Darling, and Wilf had limped hastily away from his post to warn the girl of the outlaws' approach.

'They're doing one of two things,' he said now, softly, talking for his own benefit. 'Either they're plannin' on a funeral — or they're settin' out to hunt us down.'

'But if they intend to search, why bring Ben and Hank?' Jenny whispered.

'No reason,' Wilf said, and flashed a grateful grin, knowing the girl was right.

Then he lifted a hand for silence, inched backwards so that he was looking down on the runway from the narrowest of angles.

He steadied his breathing, forced himself to remain as still as a rock while the men entered the stables, stamped their feet to clear loose mud from their boots then strode down the runway and began leading out the horses and throwing on saddles. Once there was an angry warning from a harsh voice that Gannon was able to identify as coming from the black-clad gunman. Hank Travis answered mildly, and Gannon guessed he had drifted too close to his office and the outlaws had feared he was going for his guns.

Well, that was surely close to the mark!

Then Ben Stone came into view, casually manoeuvring his horse close to the ladder while he looped the bridle over its head and got the bit into its mouth.

'Kane's going to get one hell of a shock,' he said loudly, and Gannon smiled to himself, knowing Stone was about to get across as much information as he could without being obvious enough to become suspicious. 'After more'n ten years that house of his is near ready to tumble down the hillside.'

An answer came in a voice too low for Wilf Gannon to catch. He thought he heard the sound of horses moving out into the street, leaned forward, straining to listen through the jingle of bridles, the blowing of the horses, the grunts as men strained to tighten cinches under the deliberately distended bellies of horses less than keen to leave the warm shelter of the stable.

Then his hand slipped on the edge of the opening. He lost his balance and began to topple forwards. The inside of his wrist scraped painfully across the rough edges of the boards. Top heavy, his weight was pulling him over the edge when his elbow cracked down hard on the board floor. His right elbow. As he teetered on the very edge of losing his balance and heard a rustling behind him and felt Jenny Stone's hand snatch at his belt, grasp it and hang on, the Henry was jolted out of his grasp and fell butt first towards the hard-packed floor of the runway.

The old rifle landed alongside Ben Stone. The shock of the butt slamming into the floor released the hammer. The pin slammed into the shell Wilf Gannon had jacked into the chamber and, with an almighty roar and a vivid flash, a slug tore its way through the floor of the loft.

9

Long Arrow watched with interest as the line of riders cantered away from the Circle F and turned onto the trail south.

He had approached the big ranch with caution, moving the small wagon along the grassed fringes of the trail so that most of the time it was at least partially concealed by groves of trees to which the morning mists clung tenaciously.

Eventually the unmistakable sounds of many horses moving had come faintly to his ears. He had clicked his tongue, delicately flicked the lines, and the pinto pulled the wagon tight up against the twisted oaks, came to a standstill and began to graze.

Long Arrow had said nothing to his wife and daughter, but had leaped down into the wet grass and slipped soundlessly through the trees to a point from where he had an unrestricted view of the proceedings.

Now he turned away, knowing from long experience that the heavily armed men heading towards the south constituted a posse, but a posse that had finished its business; and as he returned to the wagon and climbed back onto the seat he wondered, without undue interest, who they had been pursuing.

Five minutes later he was pulling into the Circle F, and with a wide grin Adam Flint was crossing the yard to renew acquaintance with the Indian who had taught him most of what he knew about the Bighorn country. That unstinting generosity had been rewarded many times, most recently with the gift of a chuck wagon so beat up that Wilf Gannon had treated it with contempt, but which the Indian now considered to be — as he put it — 'a damn sight roomier, but a whole heap easier for the pinto to pull' than the traditional travois.

They were drinking hot coffee in the bunkhouse, sitting with hands wrapped around hot tin cups at the end of the central table that was closest to the heat issuing in waves from the crackling pot-bellied stove.

Pleasant Ways and Smooth Skin had stayed in the wagon that had been driven into the big barn. Long Arrow had unhitched the tough little pinto, and at Flint's bidding had rubbed him down, led him to a draught-free corner and given him a feed of the best oats. The two women had acknowledged Flint's greeting with shy smiles, accepted hot drinks brought to them in the straw-smelling sweetness but declined his invitation to step down.

'I guess you make them too comfortable in that old wagon, Long Arrow,' Adam Flint said. 'Maybe have a tough time coaxing them out of it to do some work, eh?'

'Too many good men like you

offering them comfort that don't require them to lift a finger won't improve matters,' Long Arrow replied, and Mort Baxter chuckled softly at the Indian's sly riposte.

'Maybe next time I'll order them out, loan them a couple of ponies and have them out there fixing fences,' Flint said, straight-faced. 'Might even do that today, soon's they've finished their coffee.'

Long Arrow grunted. He was a man of indeterminite age, though Flint knew the story of Smooth Skin's torment at the hands of Moses Kane and guessed her father was now close to fifty. He was huddled inside an old jacket two sizes too large for him, given to him by Wilf Gannon the last time the Indian had passed through Haven. Faded denims were tucked into fringed deer-skin moccasins. His face was like leather left out in the sun to dry and crack in the heat and his long black hair was streaked with grey. But the dark eyes were like shiny creek pebbles washed by water and catching the rays of the morning sun, and his movements were sinewy grace under which lay impressive strength.

'You'd better,' he said now, 'if you're ever going to do it. After today them and me'll be a long ways out of your reach, maybe never come this way again.'

Flint raised an eyebrow and glanced quickly at Mort Baxter. 'You heading back to the Powder River?'

Long Arrow drank coffee, shook his head. 'Going south. Times have changed, most white men have become tolerant enough to make that possible. And for too long now Pleasant Ways has been pestering me to take her where the sun shines the whole twelve months of every year.'

As if to hammer home the point a cold draught washed over them as John Gray came in, stamped his feet and headed for the glowing iron stove. He brought with him the smell of damp clothing, the ranker odour of mud and wet leather. The big pot rattled metal on metal as he slipped off a glove, poured scalding coffee into a cup.

Adam Flint waited patiently until he had settled, then turned to Long Arrow and said, 'So this move south ain't got nothing at all to do with Moses Kane?'

The Indian's reaction was a sudden flaring of the nostrils as he drew in a long, measured breath, a narrowing of his black eyes as he carefully put the tin cup down and placed a hand palm down on either side of it. The deep breath was held, expelled slowly, and with some arrogance he lifted his chin in order to look hard at Adam Flint.

'Kane's here.' It was said not as a question, but as a statement, two words spoken in a flat monotone, apparently without interest; said in the quite ordinary way another man might announce the arrival of the mail, but without even that small excitement. But the eyes that looked at Adam Flint swirled with such liquid venom that it gave pause to the watching men, and for a terrible instant it was as if that hatred were directed towards them and each man there experienced a chill frisson of fear.

'You saw the posse?'

This was John Gray, and Long Arrow flicked a sideways glance at him, nodded. 'Held back, watched them ride out. Figured they'd found what they were looking for — or given up.'

'They were my men,' Mort Baxter said. 'Rode with me, anyways. Kane led a gang robbed a bank over the border in Colorado. But we'd been on their trail more than a week, finally figured out where Kane was heading. If him and his men've made it through Twin Bluffs Pass there ain't a hope in hell of prising them out of that canyon now the creek's in flood.'

'Or at any other time,' Gray said, watching the Indian. 'Given enough shells, one man with a rifle could pick off an army.'

'So we've spent some time,' Adam Flint said slowly, 'figurin' out ways in and out of High Falls Canyon without goin' through Twin Bluffs Pass.'

Long Arrow's smile was dismissive, a mere twitch of the wide mouth. 'Why? You can't get in, they can't get out. If one man can pick off an army from inside the bluffs, the three of you can do the same from outside.' His logic lay heavy on the warm air. In the silence he glanced at Mort Baxter and said, 'They've maybe got enough provisions. But if they know you are here — with or without your posse — they will spend an uncomfortable winter.'

Adam Flint cleared his throat. 'Maybe we ain't got your patience.'

The door banged open again and a puncher barged in, all bundled up in a thick coat, his Stetson pulled down low over his ears. He stopped by the end bunk and Flint scraped back his chair and went to him, and there was the murmur of conversation as the two men stood close to discuss ranch business.

Baxter crossed to the stove, lifted the coffee pot, shook it and discovered it was almost empty, then pulled a face and slammed it back down. When he sat down John Gray tossed the makings onto the table in front of him, and the burly rancher nodded his thanks and began rolling a cigarette.

The door closed again as the puncher went out. Adam Flint returned to the table, sat down, saw what Baxter was doing and with a sigh pulled out his own sack of Bull Durham.

Long Arrow had not moved.

Intently watching his own fingers at work with paper and tobacco, Adam Flint said, 'In the past fifteen years, Moses Kane's built himself a reputation. Began by stretchin' that Forty-niner's neck, went on to raise hell along the Mex border doing a certain amount of killing in a way that minimized risk to himself.'

'Killed from ambush; shot men in the back,' John Gray said bluntly. 'And word is he still has trouble keeping his hands off young women.'

The Indian's eyes flickered.

'Two of 'em in there,' Adam Flint said. He struck a match, lifted it, looked through the flame at Long Arrow. 'Bonnie Darling, Jenny Stone. Jenny's still young, dark haired, reminds me a lot of Smooth Skin . . . ' He watched for Long Arrow's reaction — about as productive as waiting for a change of expression in a stone carving, he thought wryly — then applied the dying match to the cigarette, blew a stream of smoke and said, 'When he ain't chasin' skirts, Moses Kane is likely to be passing the time gettin' even with the men he believes drove him out of the canyon, or in other ways ruined a pleasant existence — and one of the men trapped in there with that wild bunch is old Wilf Gannon.'

Long Arrow grunted, which as far as Adam Flint was concerned was the equivalent of the average man's roar of anger. He looked with satisfaction at Mort Baxter, turned back to the impassive Indian and said, 'So what I'm saying, Long Arrow, is if there is any other way into High Falls Canyon we'd appreciate your lettin' us into the secret so's we can do our best to save a few lives.'

'Wilf Gannon's a good man,' Long Arrow said.

'Right,' Adam Flint agreed, nodding.

'Since the bad times he has been like a second father to Smooth Skin.'

'Couldn't have a better — apart from your good self.'

'Also a very tough man,' Long Arrow said.

'Well now.' Flint contemplated the glowing end of his cigarette, wondered where the hell this was leading. 'Tough, sure — but like John just told you, Kane likes to shoot from cover.'

'And Wilf's pushing seventy,' John Gray pointed out.

'So,' Adam Flint said, striving to keep a tight rein on what little patience he had left, 'we reckon he needs help. But because of certain critical factors linked to the bad weather and combined with some mighty unusual geographic features — namely the bottleneck at Twin Bluffs Pass which by now has been turned into a raging torrent of white water — we're kinda hogtied.' He sucked deeply on his cigarette, tossed the glowing stub towards the stove and leaned forward to glare with some frustration into the Indian's leathery countenance.

'I'll go talk with Pleasant Ways,' Long Arrow said, and with a sinewy grace he slid away from the table, padded towards the door and walked out of the bunkhouse.

'Goddamnit!' Mort Baxter swore. 'Where in hell does that leave us?'

'Same place, and no wiser,' John Gray said. He scooped up his tobacco sack, stuffed it in his shirt pocket and rose from the table.

'You get things sorted with Merv?' he asked, referring to the puncher who had left, and when Flint nodded he said, 'I'll chase after him, send Gus along to lend a hand. Ain't no fun checking fences in this weather.'

'I guess maybe I should have got those two Injun women out after all,' Flint called after him, and Mort Baxter grinned wryly as the door slammed behind the lean foreman.

'Might have had more luck with them than old Long Arrow,' he said, 'though I surely doubt that.'

'Aw, he ain't a bad sort,' Flint said gruffly. 'I always say if there's two things I'm never, ever going to understand it's Indians and women.'

'And especially Indian women,' Baxter agreed.

'Came across enough of 'em during the war,' Adam Flint complained. 'Indian men, that is,' he added with a fleeting smile. 'Inscrutable, illogical, perverse and downright stubborn — but damn fine soldiers! I expect old Long Arrow'll come up with an answer in the end, but knowing how he likes the idea of killing his enemies through sheer boredom, likely by then the rain'll have stopped, the floodwaters' ll've gone down and there won't be any need of another way into the canyon — if there was one in the first place.'

'Well, from what I've heard, the recognized way in is about as easy to defend as Hole in The Wall,' Mort Baxter said, trickling smoke and watching his old friend through narrowed eyes. 'And what puzzles me, Adam, is if Long Arrow acted as guide when you were a newcomer in these parts, took you over every damn inch of the Bighorn Country, why isn't the alternative route down on that map you sketched?'

'Ain't there because he never showed it to me, I guess,' Flint growled. 'Hell, I was the best darned map maker in the Texas Cavalry. You know that. Would've pencilled that trail in, if there was one, but it ain't there so . . . '

His voice trailed off and, with a puzzled shake of his head he pushed away from the table, reached out to pick the coffee pot off the stove and refill his cup with coffee dregs that

126

looked as black as coal oil. When he took a mouthful, the look on his face suggested the hot, dark liquid tasted the way it looked. With a horrible grimace he puckered his lips and sprayed the entire mouthful onto the hot metal and, with a fierce hissing, white steam reeking of burnt coffee billowed into his face.

He reared back with a bellow, and was just getting into his stride, drowning Mort Baxter's guffaws with a steady stream of coarse, highly original profanity, when the bunkhouse door slammed wide open and John Gray strode in.

'Adam, if you're waiting for Long Arrow, forget it,' he called angrily. 'That goddamn useless Injun rode out of the stable large as life, set that tough little pinto buckin' like crazy in the yard then lit out, heading north. I reckon he wants Moses Kane all to himself.'

10

'Hold it!'

With the echoes of the shot from Wilf Gannon's dropped Henry repeater still ringing in his ears, Ben Stone's voice roared out. But he was a fraction late, and had nothing to back up his warning.

Outlined against the broad oblong of daylight that was the livery stable's street opening, Django Orr was a whirling black shape as he spun to one side and went for his gun. It came up in a blur of glittering metal. Orange flame spurted. A slug plucked at Stone's shirt and whined out through the back entrance.

Fractions of a second had passed. As if time had slowed to a crawl Wilf Gannon's Henry was only now toppling from the vertical.

Twice more Orr's six-gun spat flame.

Splinters flew from the timber upright alongside Stone's head. Then he leaped sideways. As he moved he plucked the lazily falling Henry out of the air. He ducked inside the nearest stall, worked the rifle's lever, sprang back out and dropped into a running crouch, snapping a wild shot at Orr as he darted across the runway.

As he rested with hands on knees in the opposite stall, panting, conscious of stabbing pains in an old back being worked too hard, he was rewarded by a yell of pain. He poked his head out, blinked through steamed-up spectacles and saw the six-gun arc into the air to fall spinning against the far wall. Again he yelled out his warning: 'Hold it, Orr, stay right where you are!' and this time the gunman straightened, stepped back a pace massaging his wrist, his face twisted with pain.

And still only seconds had passed.

Frank Tighe and Dakota Slim had ridden fast out of the livery stable, the tall man with the blind eye leading

Moses Kane's roan. Ben Stone guessed the mud was slowing them, hoped they'd got themselves in a tangle as the rattle of gunfire reached them and three horses tried to turn fast on the clogged, gluey surface.

Hank Travis was clinging onto his big bay's reins, but was backed up against the wall of the stable office where he'd stepped to stay out of the line of fire. John Darling was bent over, still clutching his dun gelding's cinch, his head turned to one side, his mouth open in shock.

The Indian was a graven statue just inside the doorway, his dark eyes inscrutable as he watched Django Orr.

'Move, Ben!' Hank Travis cried and, as he let go of the bay's reins, he slapped it smartly on the flank and sent it trotting towards the street. At the same time John Darling came out of his trance, snapped upright and forced the gelding back so that it was standing crosswise in the runway, effectively preventing a man on horseback from getting past.

Outside, a horse squealed. A man cursed loudly. From across the street Moses Kane could be heard bellowing, 'What the hell's goin' on over there!'

Then Ben Stone was clear of the stall and alongside his horse. His reaching boot found a stirrup. Still holding the Henry he grabbed the horn and swung into the saddle, touched the mare's flanks with his spurs and urged the eager animal down the runway and out the rear of the stables into the damp, icy air blowing off the roaring waters of the flooded draw.

The advantage was his. On the street side of the building Tighe and Slim were committed, had abandoned the led horse, spun their own mounts as best they could on the slick surface and urged them back towards the stables. There they were met by Hank Travis's bay trotting in the opposite direction. Precious seconds were lost in total confusion. When they eventually charged into the stables, their way was

131

blocked by Darling's gelding.

As Ben Stone swung left away from the stable and headed up the slope behind his own rooming-house, his mind was racing. The land between the eastern edge of town and the flooded draw was stony, made for fast riding, and his horse's hooves rang out in the misty air as, ears flattened, it answered Ben's urging and stretched out in a ground-eating gallop. But no more than a couple of hundred yards ahead — where the line of shacks thinned out — he would hit thick timber and be forced to swing back onto the main street.

Unarmed, at risk of being gunned down, Hank Travis and John Darling had used the confusion of the sudden burst of gunfire to feign shock and release their mounts. Ben was hoping that the tangled mess that ensued combined with Haven's main street that the rains had turned into a sloppy morass, would hinder the chase.

Pursuit would come. But already Ben had his eyes fixed on the high reaches of the canyon where the steep, timbered slopes converged until, a mile or so ahead and several hundred feet up into the hanging cloud, the way was blocked by a sheer rock fall over which there would now be cascading a tumbling mass of white water.

There was no way out. But he had been left with no other choice.

Suddenly the open land petered out as Ben reached the first stands of timber. Mist hung between the black pines like the thinning gunsmoke of a ghostly battle. He leaned forward along his horse's neck, swung hard left and rattled up between two derelict shacks to burst forth onto the upper stretch of the town's main street.

As he wheeled right and used his spurs on his horse to attack the steepening slope there was a brief period of calm in which the only sounds were the wet slap of hooves in the shallow mud, the blowing of the

133

straining mount, the background thunder of floodwater.

A shot rang out.

An insect hum sounded in Ben Stone's ear.

There was a roar of distant, impotent fury, and for fifty perilous yards Ben felt his back crawl in anticipation of the bullet that would be his finish, the chunk of hot lead that would make Jenny a widow.

Then he had reached the very fringes of the town. Here, the street regressed from a thoroughfare once much used by horses and wagons to become the original winding trail that would be ever more tightly constricted by the encroaching dark-timbered slopes. In the next hundred yards Ben left the mud-coated hardpan and, on a rutted pathway with a scattering of stones and sparse grass, he raced past the rotting timber house that had been the home of Moses Kane and — for a cruel twelve months — the Indian maiden, Smooth Skin, daughter of Long Arrow;

past the lush clearing where a line of timber uprights and peeled-pole stringers enclosed a dismal patch where headstones leaned like loose, rotting teeth.

Then he was angling upwards, heading towards the distant waterfall from which the canyon got its name, safe from the eyes of the outlaws and from their gunfire — but, ultimately, with nowhere left for him to go.

★   ★   ★

Underfoot, the loft's carpet of straw was splashed with blood.

Wilf Gannon groaned through clenched teeth. Jenny Stone clapped her hand across his mouth, eased him down to a sitting position. In the gloom her eyes were bright with alarm.

The din from below was fearful.

Someone yelled, 'Which way'd he go!'

'North,' came the swift answer. 'Rode

like the wind up the slope.'

'You were supposed to be watching them. Where the hell did that one get a gun?'

'Must've been with his saddle — ask them, they're his partners.'

Wilf grunted, settled back against the straw bale, clutched the upper part of his left arm with a right hand slippery with blood as Jenny looked intently into his eyes, took note of his affirming nod, and slowly removed her hand from his mouth.

'Ain't bad,' he said in a low, strangled voice. 'Flesh wound is all, but I'm bleeding like a stuck pig.'

She put a finger to her lips. Her eyes were calmer. Her head was tilted a little to one side, listening, as she turned partly away from Wilf, lifted her skirt and he heard the soft ripping of her petticoat.

Then her gentle fingers were unbuttoning his shirt, and his groan came again, muffled behind tight lips, as the girl eased his left arm out of the sleeve and began to attend to his wound.

'That's Moses Kane,' he murmured as another, stronger voice cut in, silencing the others.

'Too late to do anything about Stone,' Kane was saying. 'Besides, he ain't goin' nowhere. For now, get in that office, collect every weapon you can find — and when you've done that, go over these two fellers, make damn sure they don't pull another rabbit out of the hat!'

'Damnation!' Wilf Gannon muttered.

Carelessness had thrown away his one weapon, left him with a bullet hole in his upper arm and a severe case of wounded pride. Shot. By his own damn rifle!

Now he listened with frustration to the sound of hurried movement, the crash of a door opening, the thud of feet, the clash of metal on metal, and through eyes narrowed with pain he followed in his mind — a convenient distraction from Jenny's painful ministrations, he thought wryly — the unmistakable noises made by the outlaws as their thorough search took away his last chance of finding a weapon to replace his trusted Henry.

No, Wilf thought, opening his eyes wide with sudden, fierce optimism. Not the last chance, by a long chalk. There was one more, just across the street, if only the outlaws were blinded to the possibility of further weapons by those they'd discovered in Hank Travis's office. If they were, they'd send John Darling into his own mercantile for shovels, then head on up the street to resume the task they'd set themselves: to bury Dan Ford.

'Thanks, girl,' Wilf said softly. His arm still ached, but the raw pain that was like a hot knife penetrating his flesh had diminished to a dull, insistent throbbing. He reached out to touch Jenny's shoulder as she finished buttoning his shirt, and in the darkness she flashed a bright smile.

Then the smile faded, and her face once more became troubled. 'They're going,' she whispered, and Wilf nodded for, as he listened, he heard the creak of saddle leather, the jingle of bridles, the rattle of hooves on the hard runway.

'But what about Ben?' Jenny said.

Wilf forced a chuckle, under the damp white hair his face grey and tight with pain. 'Better off than he was,' he said. He pushed up and away from the bale, and as Jenny Stone reached out to steady him he made his way toward the front of the loft, took up his position against the wall.

'But there's nowhere for him to go, Wilf,' she said, as he pressed his face to the boards, squinted his eye to peer out through the narrow chink in the woodwork.

'Just a whole mountainside,' he told her reassuringly. 'And if he was to put his mind to it he could stay high in those woods, pick 'em off one by one.'

'Will he, Wilf? Will Ben do that?'

Watching the first riders move out of the stables and turn their mounts towards the up slope, he sucked his teeth, thought for a moment.

'No,' he said. 'I guess what Ben'll figure is that if he downs one of them outlaws, they'll return the compliment by plugging one of us — and I reckon that's exactly what Streak Kane'd do.'

The big outlaw with the snatched-back hair was leading the way. The two gunny sacks were once more hanging behind his saddle. He rode just ahead of Dakota Slim and Django Orr, then came Hank Travis, and John Darling leading the riderless horse. Frank Tighe was directly behind them, Winchester cradled across his thighs. The Indian, Young Fox, brought up the rear.

'We've got a chance,' Wilf said, his mind ranging far ahead. 'They'll tie Dan belly-down on that horse, collect shovels from the mercantile then ride up to the cemetery. It'll take time to dig a grave, and Kane'll want to look at that house of his. I'd say they'll be away for close on two hours.'

'But there's nothing you can do,' Jenny whispered, her breath hot on

140

Wilf's neck as she strained to watch the riders.

'Wrong,' Wilf said, his voice filled with hope. 'We'll let 'em get out of sight. Then you and me head over to the Hangdog.'

He twisted awkwardly away from the wall, fumbled to enfold both of the girl's cold hands in his big right fist, hoped she wouldn't feel its faint tremor.

'Kane and his unholy crew came to Haven without a clear idea of what they were about, Jenny. While the creek's in flood there ain't no way out for us, no way into the canyon even if anyone out there knows we're in trouble. But over at the mercantile there's guns, and ammunition. Ben's out there in the hills to the north with what's left of the Henry's shells. Down here, to the south, there's you and me — and Bonnie.'

'Yes,' Jenny said, her face suddenly alight. 'You're right, Wilf. There's a chance, isn't there; tell me there's a chance!'

'Damn right there's a chance!' Wilf said fervently. 'This thing is one hell of a long ways from being over.'

Yet even as he flashed her a grin of total, unalloyed confidence, a worm of unease was reminding him that John Darling and Hank Travis were still in the hands of the outlaws, it was pretty damn certain that somewhere, at sometime in the past, Travis and Django Orr had clashed — and, goddamn it, it was pure danged foolishness to try to out-think the outlaw Moses Kane who was not only unpredictable but was above all a merciless, cold-blooded killer.

★ ★ ★

'Take that, Wilf. John has no use for it where he is.'

They were in the kitchen behind the mercantile, which was a smaller extension of the Hangdog's. A gleaming stove stood against the back wall, a table of smoothed, scrubbed-pine planks occupied the room's centre. From one of the straight chairs placed around it a gun-belt hung, with an old Remington .44 jutting from the holster. It was this that Bonnie Darling was indicating.

Tall, angular in a straight calico dress of faded blue and with her grey-blonde hair caught back in a tight bun, she had brown eyes that were as soft as a doe's and warm lips that were forever smiling.

But today that smile was missing.

'But John'll be back,' Wilf said, and as she gave him a grim look that, more than any words, told of her disbelief, he left her to go on through into the cosy parlour and through that again into the interior of the store with its smells of sawdust and lye soap and tobaccos and the softer scents of perfumes imported from the East at a time when there were more than two females in Haven. Then, as Wilf sniffed the air, he detected with a sudden quickening of the pulse the unmistakable smell of gun oil.

143

'I'll rustle up some breakfast,' Bonnie called faintly from the back room, and in the gloom Wilf nodded absently, his eyes roving.

John Darling kept his small stock of Colt and Remington revolvers out of sight in a locked cupboard, but back of the main counter that stretched down one long wall he had a rack of repeating rifles. New Winchesters, Wilf recalled, and he limped across the dry boards, noisily sending a stack of four bright buckets clattering as he caught it with his clumsily swinging leg and was forced to thump his big right hand heavily on the shiny counter to steady himself.

The rifle rack was not locked.

Wilf selected one of the .44.40 Winchesters that the company had brought out in '73, ran his hand loving down the gleaming stock, then placed the rifle on the counter while he bent to slide open one deep counter drawer after another until he had located the boxes of shells.

When he straightened again his face was clammy with sweat, his left arm on fire.

But now he had a weapon, and he had ammunition; and, as he tucked the small, heavy cartons under his bad arm, picked the Winchester off the counter and turned to leave, he carelessly used his sleeve to dash the sweat from his lined brow — put there partly by the pain but mostly by tension — and allowed himself a thin smile of triumph.

Then the smile faded, and for several long moments he forced himself to remain still in the big, cluttered room, listening. But there were no sounds that might suggest the outlaws had changed their plans, that Moses Kane had awoken to the danger of leaving Bonnie Darling on her own and a potentially dangerous opponent on the loose. There was nothing but the soft whisper of his own breathing, the strong throb of his pulse, and from the back of the building the comforting murmur of female voices and the rattle of pans.

Wilf went out, closed the inner door behind him and made his way back through the parlour to the kitchen.

Busy at the stove, Bonnie Darling said over her shoulder, 'I don't know what you've got planned, Wilf, but before you do it this girl needs taking somewhere she can't be found.' She looked at the rifle, the boxes of shells, nodded approvingly, then tipped the sizzling pan and slid fried beef and eggs onto two tin plates.

Wilf found cutting the beef difficult with one hand, and with a tut of feigned impatience Bonnie took his plate off him, wielded her sharp kitchen knife and returned his breakfast to him with everything reduced to manageable chunks.

As he hungrily forked the tender, bloody meat into his mouth, she said, 'So far I'm the one doing all the talking, Wilf, but what I say makes sense even if Jenny doesn't agree.'

'It's just that I don't think I'm in any more danger than the rest of you,' Jenny said, fiddling with her plate. 'Those . . . those men came to Haven for a reason. Surely I'm not part of it.'

'Didn't know you were here — but if they catch a glimpse of you, it won't take them long to realize that you make an interesting and attractive diversion from the main task,' Bonnie said, her voice deliberately off-hand. 'And,' she added, 'just so we all know what we're talking about — what the heck are they here for, Wilf?'

'The general idea is to hole up for the winter with whatever loot Kane's carrying,' Wilf said, voicing an opinion he had formed as soon as he caught sight of the stuffed gunny-sacks. He nodded his thanks as Bonnie passed around steaming mugs of coffee, and put down his fork. 'But you know Moses Kane as well as I do, Bonnie. One man not a million miles from this room snuck in one dark night and took away, right from under his nose, the young Injun girl keeping his bed warm. Not too long after that a whole lot of townsfolk conspired to drive him out of his home. The massive grudge he's been harbouring must be like a festering sore inside of him.'

'You did what was right, Wilf. With the girl gone my own feeling was that Kane could and should have been allowed to remain in Haven. But others felt different, and now two of those good men who got carried along with the mob — maybe out of a firm conviction, maybe because, like all men, they didn't want to appear cowardly before their peers — two of those men just rode up that street with an outlaw holding a gun at their backs. One of them is my man, John. Both of them have got old, creaking bones, and eyes that don't see too well. And what gives me the shivers is that the place Moses Kane is leading them is Haven's cemetery.'

There was a thin scraping as Jenny Stone pushed away her plate. Her breakfast was untouched. A strand of dark hair had strayed across a cheek as pale as snow. Against that white skin her eyes were enormous.

'Your Ben is clear, and free as a bird,' Bonnie said softly, wistfully. 'Somewhere up there, safe, below the high rimrock . . . '

'With my Henry and enough shells to prove that point if they go after him,' Wilf said, grinning. 'Which they won't.' He put down his mug and covered Jenny's hand with his own big paw. He shook it gently from side to side, looked deep into those liquid eyes. 'Bonnie's right about you, girl,' he said. 'Some ways down the hill towards Twin Bluffs, set back in the trees, there's a fallen-down soddy put there by a trapper long before that old Forty-niner smelled gold, long before Moses Kane came to High Falls Canyon. I once stalked a deer up that way, came down off the far side of a low ridge and damn near fell through the dirt roof.'

Jenny shivered. 'Sounds scary,' she said, managing a tremulous smile.

'You'd be there a day, no more than that,' Wilf said.

'It'll be over that quick?' Bonnie Darling's eyes were troubled.

'One way or another,' Wilf said, nodding.

'Oh God!' Jenny Stone said in a stricken voice.

'Well,' Bonnie said, 'if trouble's that close you'd best — '

She broke off, her eyes wide, the cloth in her hand forgotten.

Like dry twigs snapping, the distant, brittle snap of two shots in quick succession came to them through the mist of morning. In the sudden, aching silence, they were followed by a third detonation so faint that had they not been holding their breath it would have gone unnoticed.

'That was Ben, using my Henry,' Wilf said bleakly.

'I know,' Bonnie said. And she sat down hard as if all the strength had gone from her legs. 'But what about the first two?'

Wilf looked at Bonnie Darling, saw a strong woman whose face had turned the colour of old, bleached bone and, taking a deep breath, he pushed his chair back from the table.

'I guess I will take that, after all,' he said. Standing as tall and straight as his bad hip would allow, moving awkwardly because of the bullet hole in his arm, old Wilf Gannon lifted John Darling's heavy gun-belt from the back of the chair and strapped it around his thick middle.

11

Before the line of riders had cleared town, John Darling had moved his horse up so that he was riding stirrup with Hank Travis.

He executed the tricky manoeuvre in some haste. He needed to speak urgently to the other man, and once they were beyond the town limits the narrow trail would make it impossible.

Under the eyes of the watchful Frank Tighe the trick was worked by deliberately sidestepping the dun, kicking it off balance so that it threw up its head and almost lost its footing on the slick mud. Darling's fight to get his own horse back on a straight course with its hooves planted was hampered when the horse carrying Dan Ford's body sheered away from the plunging dun. A quick jab of the spurs sent the dun forward, snapping the lead-rope taut, and he was alongside Travis.

'You're making hard work of a short ride,' Travis remarked drily, shaking his head as Darling proffered the makings.

'Could be the last ride we'll ever make, unless you can see some way out.'

Fishing a cheroot out of his shirt pocket, Travis shrugged. 'You figure a bullet in the back is what Kane's got planned?'

'If he ain't now, the cemetery'll sure give him ideas.'

'Him or that Django Orr,' Hank Travis said, ducking his head to light the cheroot and sneaking a fast glance back at Tighe.

Darling eyed him keenly, stowed the tobacco sack, said, 'Well?'

Travis blew a jet of pungent smoke that was whipped away by the cold wind, shook his head. 'Tighe's keeping well back, got that Winchester pointin' at your backbone. Young Fox's off to one side, lookin' casual like an Injun always looks before he takes your scalp.'

They jogged on in silence, the ground rising more steeply towards the trees, the deserted shacks thinning and finally petering out. As the street gave way to the trail and the horses' hooves began to ring musically on stone, John Darling said with desperation in his voice, 'Then the cemetery's our last chance.'

'Some chance,' Travis said bitterly, and sparks flew as he flicked away his glowing cigarette. 'Five armed men, and you and me with a shovel apiece. The Clantons had better odds than that in Arizona, and they lost.'

The wind hit them with its thin cutting edge as the trail twisted towards the west and, as the steep grassy verges encroached, John Darling was forced to drop back. He rode with his head ducked, spent some time thinking about all that had happened since Dan Ford had walked in out of the rain and had taken some good-natured joshing about protecting them from the hordes of outlaws waiting to pounce.

Well, wet night or not, they'd pounced all right. Now Dan was dead, Wilf Gannon was in hiding somewhere with Jenny Stone, Ben was up in the hills with Wilf's old rifle. And Bonnie . . .

Bonnie was OK, John Darling told himself forcefully.

She was blessed with common sense. She'd have watched them ride out, buckled on his gun-belt, saddled her horse and lit out in the opposite direction. Sure, that would take her down the long slope towards Twin Bluffs Pass. But the rain had eased hours ago, sooner or later the floodwaters would subside, and even before the pass was entirely clear the lie of the land made it possible for a courageous rider to negotiate a narrow, rocky ledge high above the raging waters.

Or maybe she'll team up with old Wilf, John Darling thought wryly. And he remembered the coolness that had grown between him and the young woman he had brought to Haven; the way, in her maturity and more frequently of late, she overtly bestowed warm glances on the old widower who walked tall still and had the physical presence to turn heads.

Some way ahead, having ridden past the ruins of his old house without turning his head, Moses Kane swung off the trail and pointed his horse up the sharp incline and into the simple enclosure where the residents of Haven buried their dead. Dakota Slim and Django Orr were close behind the big outlaw. The three men dismounted, tethered their mounts in a grove of pines that had overgrown the upslope fence poles that time and the weather had rotted.

By the time Hank Travis and John Darling rode into the cemetery leading the horse carrying the body of Dan Ford, the trio had split up and walked a little way downhill, threading their way through the low mounds of graves over which the grass and the weeds had grown, finally halting with their backs to the gravestones and crude wooden crosses.

Django Orr was in the centre, the others out wide on each flank.

And that's wrong, John Darling thought. Should be Kane in the middle, not Orr.

Then his unease was forgotten as, behind them, Frank Tighe and Young Fox, the Indian, rode in off the trail, dismounted, and loose-tethered their horses to the fence.

'Frank,' Kane called, 'stay there, face about, watch that far slope.'

At this point the canyon was no more than three or four hundred yards wide. Ever since the edge of town the slopes on either side had been closing in on the trail, quickly becoming steeper and more rugged, the atmosphere eerily grim and brooding as the mists of morning were only slowly dissipating from the branches of tall pine trees which, at this time of day, themselves seemed almost black.

So the cemetery was an unusual splash of green in a severe landscape, a man-made clearing hacked out of the forest for the sole purpose of giving the dead of Haven a decent burial.

But it seemed that decency was a long way from the mind of the outlaw Moses Kane.

As Tighe slid his Winchester out of its saddle boot, took up position alongside trees lining the cemetery's north fence and turned to look across the valley, Kane ordered Travis and Darling to dismount.

'All right,' he said, hitching his gun-belt and grinning at Django Orr. 'I guess this is where it ends.'

Hank Travis unstrapped his shovel.

'Don't bother,' Django Orr said.

Behind Travis, John Darling swore softly.

'What the hell do you intend?' Travis said. 'You gonna leave his body lyin' here for the crows?'

'His, yours . . . ' Moses Kane's dark eyes held a fiendish glitter.

For a moment Hank Travis held them with his own steady gaze. Then he drew a deep breath. 'Yeah,' he said. 'I figured as much.' In the oppressive silence he listened to John Darling's quickened breathing, said evenly, 'Do we get a chance? An even break?'

'Did I?' Moses Kane drawled.

'Is that what this is about?' John Darling said bitterly. 'A fifteen year grudge?' He spat into the grass, spread his hands in disbelief. 'You any idea how many men was involved, Kane?'

'I know two of them are standing in front of me,' Moses Kane said.

'Cut your friend down off the horse,' Dakota Slim said, his ruined eye gleaming white in the shadows. 'Then stand alongside him.'

Travis tossed the shovel aside, then took out his pocket knife and with John Darling walked over to where Dan Ford hung limp from the saddle. The horse shied, backed off, made nervous by the scent of death. Darling murmured soothingly, reached up to hold a cheek strap while Travis cut loose the body. The ostler began to ease Ford gently to the grass and John Darling released the strap, took some of the weight. Then, as Travis crouched to straighten the dead man's limbs, he moved aside to slap the horse on the flank and send it trotting away towards the fence.

Frank Tighe was leaning against a tree, chewing. The Winchester hung slack in his hand, but his head was turned as his eyes constantly raked the far slopes.

Young Fox, the Indian, had moved up the slope. He poked about among the graves, then in the pine-scented shadows sank down into an easy squatting position and become as one with the weathered headstones.

Hank Travis looked up at John Darling, saw grey eyes devoid of hope and shook his head. Their only weapons had been the heavy, sharp-bladed shovels. They were thirty yards downslope from the half-circle of armed outlaws, fifty from the nearest horse.

Travis took a last, long look at Dan Ford, then climbed stiffly to his feet.

As he did so, from behind them there came the oily click of a pistol being cocked.

⋆   ⋆   ⋆

Ben Stone was still on the western side of the canyon.

He was there because the floodwaters thundering down the wide, stony wash from High Falls made it impossible for a man to cross to the far slopes. But the tortuous nature of the vast box-canyon was such that half a mile north of the cemetery the deep chasm that was like a wound cutting into the Bighorns took a lazy curve towards the east before swinging back to its northern orientation. Although he was on the same side of the canyon as the riders, its eastward swing meant that from trees bordering a high, rocky outcrop, Ben Stone was able to see Moses Kane's big blue roan crest the rise at Haven's northern edge.

161

He had slipped Wilf Gannon's Henry from its scabbard, then left his horse and threaded his way swiftly down through the thick silence of the pines to a flat slab of jutting rock from where he could watch the column wend its way up the twisting trail from town.

From that position he could also look directly down on the cemetery. Now, he watched intently as the horsemen rode in, dismounted and took up their positions, and with his mind washed clear of all illusion by his own frantic ride to freedom through the cold morning air — and the reasons that lay behind it — what he was seeing only confirmed his worst fears.

This was no ordinary burial party.

From his high vantage point to the north of the small, grassy enclosure — somewhat poetically, Jenny Stone had once looked at Ben with shining eyes and told him that it was the Lord's corral for the souls of the dead — he saw the three gunmen form their loose half circle; watched with a deep sense of loss as his two friends cut down the body of Dan Stone; and with a tightening of his jaw muscles, he saw the black clad gunman, Django Orr, dip his hand to his holster.

With a muttered oath Ben Stone settled himself against a jutting hunk of rock, and with a quick prod of his finger to settle his spectacles he lifted the Henry to his shoulder.

* * *

Bellies tight with sudden fear, their back muscles involuntarily clenched against the expected agony of a bullet, the two men turned about.

Django Orr's six-gun was drawn and cocked and tilted nonchalantly with the hammer under the heel of his thumb. His legs were apart. The sweat of sudden high tension glistened on his face. He swung his head towards Moses Kane as if looking for a signal, and the conchos in his hat glittered as a weak sun appeared through the thinning cloud.

'Don't I know you?' Hank Travis asked.

Orr's voice was taut with excitement. 'Maybe. A long time ago, a long ways from here,' he said. 'San Antone, Laredo.' He shrugged dismissively, his mind fixed on the gun in his hand, the two helpless old-timers. 'A bar somewhere, the small matter of a woman . . . '

'Always is,' Travis said.

'Was,' Moses Kane said. 'Your time's up.'

'In that case,' Travis said wearily, 'tell him to pull the goddamn trigger.'

'I got me a better idea,' Django Orr said slyly. 'Why don't we let Young Fox do it, with his beeg peeg sticker?'

Over by the far gravestones overhung by dark pines, Young Fox came lithely to his feet. 'No, my friend, the knife is for you.'

Orr snorted contemptuously and flashed a wolfish grin at the watching Dakota Slim. 'You're a woman, Young

164

Fox, ain't that right, Slim? All he's good for is running along with the squaws when the fightin's finished, usin' that blade to slit the throats of helpless soldiers.'

'That would seem to make you safe,' Young Fox reasoned. 'To be a soldier a man needs the guts to fight against armed men.' He watched the pale face twist in an angry snarl, coolly measured the slim black figure, his dark eyes unreadable. 'But maybe, in your case, I make an exception.'

'You're both wasting time,' Moses Kane said flatly, 'and with two men on the loose, time's what we ain't got too much — '

Suddenly, shockingly, his words were cut short. The air above John Darling's head was parted with a fast whirring sound and something smacked hard into a headstone directly behind Django Orr and whined off into the trees. It was followed almost instantly by the flat crack of a rifle.

The shot was like a signal releasing

165

Hank Travis and John Darling from invisible bonds. With its fading echoes still rippling along the rimrock Darling turned and took half-a-dozen desperate, lumbering strides across the grass towards the tethered horses. Without hesitation Hank Travis exploded forwards and began a powerful, lunging run directly towards Django Orr.

Splinters of stone were still flying like hot needles as Moses Kane flung himself belly-down behind the nearest headstone.

Young Fox melted back into the shadows under the trees.

Off to one side, Dakota Slim spun. His hand dropped to his thigh and came up holding his sixgun. He lifted his face towards the sound of the shot. Out of the corner of his eye, he caught John Darling's swift movement. With deceptive speed the six-gun flicked sideways. He snapped a single shot. Darling grunted as if in surprise. His thick legs went from under him. He dropped heavily to his knees, toppled forwards onto his face and, like a bulky log, began to roll down the slope.

Django Orr waited until Hank Travis was less than ten feet away and still running. Then the six-gun bucked in his fist. Travis jerked as if he'd run into a wall. He took another faltering step towards the gunman then stopped. Somehow his dying brain found the intelligence to send his hand reaching towards his right hip. It got there, pawed helplessly at the cloth of his pants, found no gun. But he was unaware of its absence. His head fell forward. Like a man whose bones have turned to water, he collapsed in a shapeless heap.

Django Orr's glittering eyes raked the clearing. He looked at Dan Ford; at the hatless figure of John Darling lying further down the slope, bald scalp gleaming; at Hank Travis, who had got so close he had died with his floppy grey hair brushing the toes of Orr's black, mud-caked boots. Then the smoking six-gun became a glittering, spinning blur in the killer's hand, smacked into its holster, and he turned and leaped for cover.

He was that fraction of a second too late that marks the difference between living and dying.

Both feet were off the ground when there was the sound of a cleaver hitting meat and the second shot from the high slopes took him in the back. He jerked in the air, arched, flung both arms wide. When he came down his legs tried to run, but it was a dying reflex. He fell awkwardly, his head cracking against a headstone. The concho-studded black hat spun away. Django Orr lay on his back, one leg twitching.

Then, from the northern fringe of trees, Frank Tighe opened up with his Winchester. Momentarily fazed by the action behind him, he had turned in time to spot the second muzzle flash and now he angled the rifle sharply upwards to blast a series of shots towards the wisp of gunsmoke.

A figure rose, darted from the cover

168

of a jagged boulder and sprinted across the rock slab.

Tighe grunted with satisfaction. He took careful aim, fired. High above them there was a wink of bright light as a falling rifle caught the sun, bounced, arced high to spin lazily towards the lower slopes. Then the figure, now bent over and moving sluggishly like a man waist-deep in fast river water, had reached the shelter of the pines.

Behind the tall headstone, Moses Kane swore viciously. Dakota Slim was through the back fence and in amongst the horses, belatedly dragging his rifle from its saddle boot.

The echoes of the last shot died away, lost in the high rimrock.

Then Young Fox, the Indian, was padding across the grass. As he ran he drew his knife. The cold metal flashed in the weak sunlight. He reached Django Orr, sank down on one knee by the dying gunman, looked into the staring black eyes and said softly, 'You know, my friend, maybe you were right,

169

after all. I am a woman. You are a dying soldier. I do what must be done.'

And with a single sweep of the broad blade he slashed Django Orr's throat.

In the heavy silence bright red blood gushed out to stain the crisp green grass.

★　★　★

A harsh gasp of agony was torn from his throat.

With his back against the rough trunk of a tall pine and his eyes turned sightlessly towards the sky, Ben Stone sat with legs outstretched and used a piece of sharp stone to slash through the blood-soaked cloth of his pants.

The bullet had entered the back of his left thigh and ploughed through flesh and muscle. As far as he could tell no artery had been hit, but blood was flowing freely, forming a thickening pool on the bed of pine needles.

Ben Stone lowered his head, forced his eyes to focus, clamped his teeth to hold back a low moan.

He had slashed away the cloth on the front and back of his thigh. Where the slug had entered there was a dimple as big as the tip of his finger; the exit hole was a bloody, ragged tear in bleeding flesh. Ben used the jagged stone to cut right around his pants leg, bit into his lower lip against the agony as he used his right foot to prise off his left boot, then slipped the severed pants leg down and off over his foot.

With trembling fingers he yanked his shirt out of his belt, slashed off a rough square, cut that section in half and formed two thin pads. He left smears of blood on his throat as he slipped off his bandanna and used it to hold the pads over the gaping wounds in his thigh, wrapping it around once, tightly, then holding it in place with his hand.

Then he fell back, gasping.

It took most of his remaining strength to secure the makeshift bandage with a crude knot. When he looked up the steep slope his horse was visible

171

through the pines, its rich chestnut coat shining in the dappled light no more than a hundred yards away. The horse was tethered to a tree. As Ben blinked and peered through his spectacles, his eyes fogged with pain, he thought he could see the glint of the patient animal's eyes, and guessed it was looking in his direction.

Ben Stone squeezed his eyes tight shut, took a deep, ragged breath.

He was unarmed, bleeding like a stuck pig, and Moses Kane might take it into his head to come after him.

But whether he did or not was of no consequence.

Ben knew he couldn't reach his horse.

And if he didn't, one way or another he would die before nightfall.

12

By the time the sun broke through and began to disperse the mist hanging low over the plains, Adam Flint had led John Gray and Mort Baxter as far as the towering cliffs of Twin Bluffs Pass. There, with the roar of the tumbling waters loud in their ears, they turned off the wide muddy trail onto a slope of short buffalo grass leading up to an expanse of jagged scree. When they drew rein in a grove of gnarled, stunted trees their mounts were close to being wrung out, coats streaked with white lather, heads drooping from the cruel pace.

'At this rate we'll kill 'em,' Mort Baxter said bluntly. All three horses were carrying loaded saddle-bags and booted rifles; all three riders were big-framed and well covered with hard muscle. Baxter's own mount had been a hard week on the trail. He knew that a few hours' rest had not been enough to restore its strength.

'Scout around, John,' Adam Flint said, grunting as he stooped to loosen a cinch. 'Ground's so soft after that rain decipherin' tracks'll be as easy as thumbin' through a picture book.'

He watched the tall foreman head off downslope towards the flatter ground leading to the pass, then turned and squinted at Baxter. 'You want your cash, Mort,' he said. 'I'm intent on saving lives. If succeeding in both those aims costs a couple or three good horses, well, it's a price worth paying — but, hell, you don't need to listen to me preaching. You and that posse could've stayed at home drowning your sorrows. Instead you chased those killers clear across Wyoming Territory. Would've caught 'em, too, if the weather hadn't turned.'

Mort Baxter stood with hands on hips, easing his aching back, watched John Gray some hundred yards away,

174

cutting back and forth across the trail. 'Heard of Indians tracking white men,' he mused. 'Can't say I've heard of white men trackin' Indians with too much success.'

Flint laughed. 'Most times I'd agree with you. But just like your mercantile friend in the posse put a name to an outlaw and made it easy for you to figure out where he was headed, all John's doing is confirming what I already know: Long Arrow's heading west. Has to. The town of Haven's built on the west side of them floodwaters. If there is a way into the canyon from the rimrock it has to be down the western slopes.'

'Otherwise we'd be on the wrong side of the waters, lookin' across at Kane and his cronies but as far away from them as ever.' Baxter nodded, and said, 'A hell of a place to build a town, Adam.'

As John Gray walked back up the slope towards them Flint said, 'Well, in the first place, it was never intended to *be* a town. Moses Kane settled there for his own damn reasons, one of which was a need to disappear after he got caught raping a white woman over in the Nations. Then that crazy miner rode in on his mule, sniffed the piny air and scented gold, and in the space of three months the place went from one house to half a hundred shacks and a couple of stores.'

John Gray reached them, and Flint said, 'The way we figured it, John?'

Spattered with mud after following Flint's horse from the Circle F, Gray was looking disgruntled and breathing hard; like most range men he was unaccustomed to walking, and his boots had made it tough work. He spat, went to his horse and dragged a canteen out of his saddle-bags, took a quick pull of water and spat again.

'They rode up into the canyon all right. Stayed out of the water till they got close to the pass, then were forced to ride through it.' He stowed his canteen, took a calculating look at the tumbling water. 'I'd guess they made it in the nick of time — and as far as I could make out from that mess of tracks in the mud there was no more than three of 'em. That make sense, Mort?'

For a few moments Mort Baxter mulled over the information, building a smoke while he let his eyes range the landscape.

Over the years the winter floodwaters pouring through the pass from High Falls Canyon had cut a deep arroyo that ran due south from the cliffs. Dry and dusty for most of the year, by November it was transformed into a ravine through which a muddy river ran fast and deep. At such times it was impossible to imagine it any other way, and their only route across from east to west had been some miles south where the waters were slowed by distance and began to spread. They had been able to walk their horses easily through a wide, shallow ford where the waters swirled no more than hock deep.

Streak Kane would have done the same, in darkness, with icy, wind-driven rain soaking him and his men as they rode through the black night.

But Kane was no fool. With a posse at his heels he was forced to move fast, yet without prior knowledge he had no way of telling which way Haven had gone in the fifteen years he'd been away. The most likely was a slow drift into decline, the wild brush reclaiming the land the miners had ripped from it with pick and shovel and the sweat of hard, futile work.

If Haven had prospered, then a growing population might have found the need for a lawman . . .

'Yeah, he must've sent a couple of men on ahead,' Baxter said with some disquiet, and he blew a stream of smoke and looked at Adam Flint. 'But would a ghost town have need of a constable, Adam?'

'A bunch of old-timers, with old-timers' ideas.' Flint's smile was warm at the thought. 'People like that do things

178

right, Mort, so one of 'em runs the store, another the rooming-house, a feller called Hank Travis has the stable and old Dan Ford, he struts around with a badge pinned to his shirt.'

Baxter pulled in a deep breath that swelled his broad chest. He shook his head, his face grim. 'Then if it happened the way I figure it, we're some hours too late. But that don't mean we can waste time. You cut any Indian sign, John?'

'One rider rode hard across country, angled away from Twin Bluffs, likely heading for the foothills a mile or so west of here.' Gray smiled thinly. 'If you want his name I'll need to get a mite closer.'

'Which is exactly what we intend to do,' Adam Flint said. He whistled shrilly, and when his horse's head came up and it lazily ambled his way he shocked it out of its drowsiness by walking to meet it and jerking tight the slack cinch. That done, he swung his lean frame up into the saddle.

'Haven's a town that went to sleep

more than ten years ago,' he said, wheeling and backing his horse impatiently as the others tightened cinches and swung over leather. 'Chances are those scouts he sent on ahead will've caught the old-timers by surprise. Whether or not, when Kane gets there he'll be all tuckered out, and even a good man ain't got much patience when his eyes feel like they're full of grit.' His sudden scowl turned his blue eyes to ice. 'That don't give me much hope for Wilf Gannon and his pals, because Streak Kane was born bad clear through.'

He jerked at the reins, pulled the skittish horse around towards the west and touched it lightly with the spurs. As he moved off at a fast canter, Mort Baxter spoke to his own horse and quickly drew alongside, a frown on his face.

'The Indian's too far ahead, and without him we're stumped,' he said. 'Even with Long Arrow we're outnumbered by cold-blooded killers, the stolen cash ain't going nowhere until spring and odds are your man's already dead. Ain't this a waste of time?'

'Maybe.' Flint looked across at John Gray keeping pace some way off on his left flank, called, 'What about Long Arrow, John?'

Hat brim flattened back by the breeze, Gray turned and gave a shake of his head. 'If he's after Kane for himself, we won't catch him.'

'And if he isn't?'

Gray waved a hand vaguely. 'He told Pleasant Ways and Smooth Skin where he was going — but, hell, he would do that, wouldn't he?'

'An Indian never does anything without good reason,' Adam Flint said. 'And, as I recall, you mentioned that before he rode out of the yard he put on a show of fancy riding with that pinto. I think the old devil wants help, John, and if my hunch is right he's up there now with his ear to the ground and laughing fit to bust.'

And with a flashing grin Flint raked

his horse's flanks and streaked away along the edge of the foothills at a fast gallop.

⋆　⋆　⋆

It was approaching midday when Adam Flint called a halt.

They'd ridden hard across open country for several miles, then cut north and headed for the high ground; the going had got tougher as the grassy slopes became progressively steeper. As they entered thickening timber where the light from the hazy sun filtered down onto a carpet of leaves and pine needles and rock shelves slippery with moss, they were forced to search for trails, frequently slowing their horses to a walk or dismounting to lead them along deep gullies edged with loose boulders where riding was a perilous business for both horses and men.

But what rankled more than anything else was that after three or four miles of climbing into the high country they were forced to admit they were riding blind. Each man knew that High Falls Canyon lay a couple of miles to the east, that the canyon narrowed as it penetrated deeper and higher into the Bighorns, and that at its inner end a box was formed by towering cliffs and the thunderous cascade of High Falls.

But early in the push north they had all agreed that swinging east to hit the canyon's rimrock would make the ride infinitely more hazardous and — though the likelihood was remote — would put them at risk of being spotted by outlaws whose life of crime made them unceasingly vigilant.

By Adam Flint's reckoning, they were now level with the inner end of the winding box canyon. And though it was now futile to continue on their present course — which would only take them deeper into the rugged mountain country beyond the furthest reaches of High Falls Canyon — the alternative was ruled out because without Long

Arrow they had no way of reaching Haven.

So, as the three men came together in the centre of the clearing, their eyes probed the deep shadows cast by the encircling woods for what each of them reluctantly acknowledged might be the last time. Long Arrow's show of bravado as he rode out of the Circle F had been not an invitation, nor even a challenge; it had been a gesture of contempt for three white men who, in his eyes, were incapable of helping their own kind.

'Decision time,' Mort Baxter said. He was leaning forward in the saddle, hands folded over the horn, Stetson pushed back from his damp grey hair.

'With only one choice, that ain't hard,' John Gray said. His lean face was patient, his eyes constantly alert.

Adam Flint was some way off, walking his horse around the perimeter of the clearing. Now he shook his head in an admission of defeat and cut back across the springy turf to join the others. Angrily, he jerked the makings from his shirt pocket and began to fashion a cigarette.

'I'll go along with that,' he said, 'and in addition, Mort, I'll give you a belated answer to your question. Yes, this is a goddamn waste of time. More than that, it's a *criminal* waste of time, because while we're chasin' our tails in these woods there's men not more'n a couple of miles over yonder must be gettin' pretty desperate.'

A match flared as Flint finished making his cigarette, and the aroma of tobacco smoke mingled with the rank smell of wet vegetation and the stink of the lathered sweat coating the hard-pressed horses.

'So what we should have done right from the start is rode up the rim of the canyon in the hope of finding a way down,' Baxter said.

'No. Maybe. Aw, hell . . . ' Flint swore softly at his own indecision. 'I tell you, Mort, I just don't know. All I do know is doing it this way has achieved

185

nothing, and we've lost a couple of hours. That ain't much to us, but to Wilf Gannon it could've made the difference between staying alive or gettin' his old hide plugged full of holes.'

'What Mort said makes sense, Adam,' John Gray said quietly. 'And if you look at it logically, you'll see that although we didn't ride up the canyon rim, we've lost nothing.' He eased his weight in the saddle, tipped his head in the direction of the canyon. 'We'd have ridden this far anyway. All we've done is the same ride, in the same direction, but a couple of miles to the west.'

'And since we've come this far . . . ' Flint nodded slowly, killed the cigarette, flicked it away. 'I suppose one way of gettin' to Haven is to slide all the way down through them woods on our backsides . . . '

'Sure take those outlaws by surprise,' Mort Baxter said, suddenly grinning.

'And that,' John Gray said, 'is the only way any good is going to come of this. Because if we do make it down, we'll be on foot, at best nursing sprains and bruises, certainly outnumbered and outgunned by men who stay alive through their skill with Sam Colt's favourite toy. But . . . if all that ain't made you think twice . . . '

He looked at his companions, saw the pained look in two pairs of eyes and turned away with a grin.

Flint clicked his tongue and pointed his horse towards the east. As the others wheeled their mounts to follow him and he led the way across the grass and up out of the clearing, he said casually, 'Maybe one or two of those fellers down there have worked a trick or two. Old never did mean useless, and if Moses Kane had that notion when he rode in could be they surprised him.'

And then he was leaning forward in the saddle. Reins held high he urged his straining horse up the steep slope out of the small basin. With a crash of brush it crested the narrow ridge and leaped down the short slope into the thickening trees.

Then Adam Flint swore softly.

'And talking of surprises,' he said with awe in his voice, 'here's one for us that ain't exactly unwelcome.'

As he again eased back, the following horses bunched and jostled behind him, bridles jingling and saddles creaking as Baxter and Gray sawed on the reins.

Then they too were stunned into silence.

Ahead of them, caught in a shaft of sunlight, the Sioux, Long Arrow, sat astride his pinto, his old Sharps resting butt down on his thigh and pointing like a lance towards the blue morning skies.

13

While Wilf fretted and drank a last cup of lukewarm coffee, the women disappeared into Bonnie's bedroom to discard their dresses in favour of serviceable work shirts and pants tucked into riding boots.

That done they left the mercantile and crossed the expanse of drying mud to the livery stable, Wilf lugging a sack of supplies, Bonnie with a couple of long guns cradled in her arms and a gun-belt slung over her shoulder, facts which had Wilf puzzled as much as her change of clothing but only in that small part of his mind that wasn't occupied with the more important task of sniffing the air for the scent of danger.

So in the familiar gloom he saddled two horses — at Bonnie's instigation because, she said, she wanted to see

Jenny settled — and with a last, wary glance towards the top end of town they headed out, the women riding double as Wilf led the way south. Some way out of town he squinted up at the sun, measured what he saw against the long shadow of a solitary pine then turned off the trail to set his horse climbing the western slopes.

When they were well into the trees he slowed, poked a finger under his hat to scratch his head, looked about him for a while to confirm what he'd already figured from the sun and the shadows and what was left of his memory, then urged the horse forwards and took them unerringly the half-mile or so through the tall trees and wet under-growth covering the steep side of the canyon to the high fold on the far side of which the old trapper's hut nestled.

Below it the land sloped sharply downwards. A little way above, the soft wet earth finally gave way to hard rock shelves which marked the end of the tree line, and beyond, on the other side of a narrow band of loose scree bathed in bright, unrestricted sunlight, the cliffs rose sheer to the rimrock.

'Ain't nothing to bother you here,' Wilf said, as Jenny slid down from behind Bonnie and gazed apprehensively at the ruined pile of rotting timber and tar-paper that was almost lost in the thick blanket of dead leaves and rampant undergrowth. 'No reason on earth why any of those fellers'd head in this direction. And by nightfall, one way or another this'll be finished.'

I'm beginning to repeat myself Wilf thought with wry amusement, and I guess like memory loss that's a sign of age. And then even that notion was dismissed to the small section of his brain set aside for the storing of useless information because, when they handed Jenny the saddle-bags packed with cold food and two canteens of water and she had stowed them inside the tumble-down shack and come outside again to sit on a mossy log in the warm, dappled sunlight, Wilf suddenly realized the

191

greater implications of Bonnie's cargo of weapons, and her insistence on a second horse.

She wasn't just riding to see Jenny settled out of harm's way: it was her intention to take an active part in the fight against the outlaws led by Moses Kane — and Wilf knew that with this self-willed woman there was nothing he could do that would stop her.

So when Bonnie swung into the saddle, a Winchester jutting from under her right leg, a brand new Colt at her hip and a Greener shotgun resting across her thighs, Wilf cast one hard glare in her direction, then set his jaw and wheeled his horse to ride recklessly down the long slope.

Two hectic minutes later he stopped in the trees some way short of the trail and waited for Bonnie to catch up, breathing hard, brushing broken twigs from his shirt while nursing his aching arm, and realising with disgust that he was acting like an old fool.

Wilf reckoned he'd come across some

stubborn critters in his life, most of them longhorns, burros or mules. From time to time his wife had dug her heels in over one thing or another, but usually Wilf had been able to talk her round or come to a compromise, more often than not when the oil lamp had been blown out and the darkness and the warmth of their bed made everything else seem unimportant.

But Bonnie wasn't his wife. And with the likelihood of Moses Kane and his men already heading back to town they had no time for protracted arguments.

'I'll say it once, then it's finished,' he said, as she rattled up behind him, face flushed but set in a grim mask of determination. 'What's about to happen ain't woman's work. I'd sooner see you safe in the mercantile till it's over — better still, up on the hillside with Jenny — but as you've chose to do it this way . . . ' He shrugged, and cracked a thin smile that showed undisguised disapproval mixed with admiration he found impossible to keep hidden.

'That said,' Bonnie murmured, looking at him with steady brown eyes, 'let's get our heads together and figure out how we're going to handle this. We heard shots, what, thirty minutes ago? Those outlaws must have moved since, and as there's only one way they could go they must have been pretty close to town even as we left.'

'I reckon,' Wilf said. He thought for a moment, then went on, 'But there's really no need for us to go up against them. Just like Jenny, we can get lost in this canyon. The floodwaters'll be down in three or four days, all three of us can ride out, head for Adam Flint's Circle F . . .'

From the set of her jaw as she listened he knew he was wasting his breath. With a shake of his head he said, 'All right, have it your way. I'll admit with all that weaponry you're totin' I'm kinda glad to have you along, but there's still five of them, and just us two.'

'If those shots mean what we think they meant.'

He moved his horse alongside hers, reached out to touch her arm. 'I'm sorry,' he said gruffly. He saw the pain in her eyes, said, 'I wish I could give you some hope, but I was there in the Hangdog, watched Django Orr enjoy gunning down Dan Ford. And we both know that Moses Kane is a merciless killer nursing one hell of a grudge.'

'For now, forget Hank and . . . and John. Are you saying there's no hope for us?'

Wilf rubbed his chin, absently felt the scrape of whiskers, and when he looked at Bonnie Darling there was a gleam in his eyes. 'I know this canyon,' he said with a tremor in his voice. 'Better than most, though not good enough to get us out of here. But there's trails — like this one — all over the hillside, some of 'em made by Injuns, some by miners, some of 'em game trails been there since the beginning of time. We can use them,

Bonnie, you and me. Ain't no need to ride into town, tackle those fellers head on . . . '

'Guerrilla warfare,' Bonnie said, and she turned to gaze up into the high country as if seeing the picture he had painted. 'Is that what you're saying, Wilf?'

'You've got it,' he said. 'Hit 'em, then fade away only to come back and hit 'em again.'

'And Ben Stone?' Bonnie asked. 'Does old Ben figure in this?'

Wilf narrowed his eyes in speculation.

'Somewhere out there in the hills, behind them, with my Henry,' he said at last. 'His eyes ain't too good — but maybe Ben's our hole card, Bonnie.'

'I'd like to think so,' Bonnie said, and the Greener's barrel glinted in the sun. 'I'd like to believe that what you have planned will work. We've got to play the hand as it's been dealt to us, Wilf, I know that. But I have a feeling the cards we've got may not be good enough. We need three men like Ben up in the hills, Wilf, three hole cards,' she said with a grim smile. 'And if you and me are going to come out of this alive, every one of them'll need to be aces.'

* * *

At the top end of High Falls Canyon, four horsemen sat to one side of a vast chasm and gazed down on waters that had begun as heavily falling rain lashing the rock some 9,000 feet up Cloud Peak, been swelled by countless other converging streams that danced and gurgled from rock to rock as they tumbled from the heights of the Bighorns, and now, as a mighty, rushing torrent of black water, tumbled dizzily into space to fall with a thunderous roaring onto the smooth rocks some hundred feet below sending clouds of spray drifting like white smoke on the swirling breeze.

From the rocky, tree-lined canyon-side, three of the men gazed into the cauldron of white water with awe. The fourth sat astride his pinto lower down the slope and watched without a flicker of emotion on his seamed face but with eyes that were deeply amused.

'Down there?' Adam Flint demanded loudly over the roar of the falls, his eyes narrowed as he looked across at Long Arrow. 'You telling us that's the way into the canyon?'

'The only way,' Long Arrow affirmed.

'And you brought us here for this madness?' John Gray said with disbelief.

Long Arrow shrugged. 'Did I bring you?'

'Hah!' Flint backed his nervous horse away from the crumbling edge, said curtly, 'You know you did. But if you wanted us with you, why ride out alone?'

'It was a beginning,' Long Arrow explained. 'I could have waited, but when action is needed white men talk too much about nothing.'

'Goddammit!' Mort Baxter swore, 'all Flint was askin' was for you to show us the way into the canyon.'

'Talk too much, and don't always mean what they say, or what they write on useless pieces of paper,' Long Arrow added pointedly.

'Do Indians?' Flint said with a challenging glare.

Long Arrow's mouth twitched in what could have been a smile. 'Indians always mean what they say. It's just that most white men don't understand what the Indian means.'

'And if that ain't wastin' time with useless talk,' John Gray said in disgust, 'I'll eat my hat.'

This time Long Arrow did smile. 'You're right,' he said. Digging his moccasined heels lightly into his pony's flanks he spun the horse and galloped swiftly away down the narrow grassy slope between the trees and the sheer drop into High Falls Canyon. After fifty yards the slope dropped sharply, the trees closed in, and the grass gave way to flat slabs of rock and jutting outcrops that appeared to hang over the canyon.

The racing pony's hooves clattered on the hard surface.

'Jesus!' Mort Baxter breathed.

Then, as sunlight glistened on the sleek, dappled coat of the Sioux's pony, its rider sat up straight and hauled on the halter. The pinto gave a high-pitched whinny and slid on braced legs, almost sat back on its haunches and, as its forelegs pawed the air, Long Arrow twisted his body to one side and hauled the horse around towards the canyon's rim.

With a jab of his heels he urged it forwards in what appeared to be a suicidal lunge towards the downslope side of a massive, weathered boulder.

And then he was gone.

For a moment it was as if all the sounds in the world had been hushed, all movement stilled. Then, faintly, so disembodied that they were without direction, the listening men heard the sound of receding hoofbeats.

'On foot, I'd think about it,' Adam Flint breathed. 'But that Injun's just gone straight over the edge, on horseback.'

'You heard him,' John Gray said, flicking the reins and moving off down the slope after Long Arrow. 'We talk too damn much.'

★ ★ ★

'You just cut Django Orr's throat — and now you're walking out?'

Down on one knee, Young Fox wiped the blood off his knife on the downed outlaw's black shirt then looked up at Kane and shook his head. 'Orr was already dead.'

'Let him go,' Dakota Slim called, walking down the slope leading the horses. 'With Orr out of the way we're already on a four way split, 'stead of five. Young Fox goes, we split three ways.'

'Sure,' Frank Tighe urged, his eyes shining with avarice. He was breathless, proud of his shooting, sure he'd winged the distant rifleman. 'We're up against one old man and a couple of women. We don't need no Injun.'

'Nobody walks out on me,' Kane insisted. He was standing over the Indian. A muscle twitched in his jaw.

'Up to now,' Young Fox said, and stood up.

'What makes now any different?'

'This.' Young Fox held up his knife. It was balanced lightly in his sinewy fingers. Sunlight flashed on the broad blade.

'Well now . . . ' Kane began. And then his voice died.

The knife seemed to flicker as it came down. It parted Kane's shirt front with a whisper of sound, continued down to slice through his thick leather gun-belt, then whipped back up to finish with the needle-sharp point pricking Kane's bulging Adam's apple.

In the sudden silence the outlaw's twin six-guns hit the ground with a dull thud.

'Now, that beats anything I ever saw,'

Dakota Slim marvelled, amusement in his voice.

'Unbuckle your gun-belt,' Young Fox said, the knife steady at Kane's throat. 'And you, Tighe.'

'It's your play,' Slim said amiably, and with a swift movement he stripped the belt from around his lean waist and let it fall. With a shrug, Frank Tighe followed suit.

'Now tell Tighe to bring my horse,' Young Fox told Kane.

Kane turned his head and spat. The knife point shifted on his throat, drawing a droplet of bright blood.

'Not me, kid. You want it, you ask.'

Dark Indian eyes met those of the white killer, revealed nothing but an implacable patience. A horse blew softly. A bird called raucously, high in the trees.

Young Fox reached out, twisted his left hand in Kane's ruined shirt. He bent his elbow, pulled the outlaw onto the knife. The droplet of blood became a dark trickle leaking into damp chest hairs.

Beads of sweat burst forth on Moses Kane's brow. Voice ragged with hate he said, 'Fetch his horse, Frank.'

'Hell, Mose — !'

'Do it!'

'Don't even think of going for one of those rifles, Slim.' Young Fox looked across Kane's shoulder, watched the tall man with the ruined eye flash a grin then reach up a hand to gentle a horse that had sensed the tension and begun to toss its head. Its uneasiness was picked up by the others, and all three horses began to move restlessly so that Dakota Slim had his hands full clutching the reins.

A moment later Frank Tighe was back with the Indian's lean mustang.

Young Fox's face wore a thin smile. Without a change of expression he released the bunched shirt, took the knife from Kane's throat and gripped the blade with his strong white teeth. Then he stepped swiftly away from the outlaw and in one fluid movement

204

swung onto the horse's bare back and kicked it in the ribs.

As the horse lifted its head and leaped away, Kane dropped to his knees. He fumbled with the looped gun-belt and clumsily drew a .45. When he came up with the pistol cocked, Young Fox was racing his horse up the slope. He took it on a jinking, weaving course through the tangle of headstones. By the time the first shot cracked he was over the rotted fence. When Moses Kane's hammer finally clicked on an empty chamber and the rattle of gunfire died away the Indian was an indistinct blur heading uphill through the dark pines.

'Now what the hell has that achieved?' Dakota Slim asked obscurely, and his blank eye swivelled towards Moses Kane.

'Shut your goddamn mouth, Slim.'

Kane tossed aside his slashed belt, bent down to unbuckle Django Orr's gun-belt, in his fury heaving the dead man bodily off the ground as he wrenched the belt free and buckled it around his own waist.

'We do it this way,' he said and his face was a mottled white under its tan, his eyes raging. 'We ride back to town. We go through every goddamn shack, one by one. We find Wilf Gannon we kill him. Then we find the women . . . '

'I got me a bad feeling,' Tighe said uneasily. 'Ain't nothing gone right since we rode in. Now that tricky redskin's on one side of us, Gannon on the other, maybe got us in his sights right now.'

But already he was talking to Kane's back. The big outlaw strode across the grass, snatched the reins from Dakota Slim, swung into the saddle and with a jab of the spurs sent his horse hammering down the slope towards the trail.

With a shrug of resignation, Dakota Slim recovered his gun-belt and followed suit. As he moved off after Kane he reached down to slide his Winchester out of its boot, jacked a shell into the breech and rested the rifle across his thighs.

When he turned onto the trail his head was never still as his good eye ranged the high slopes on both sides of the canyon.

Frank Tighe was last out of the cemetery. He left behind him four horses peacefully grazing, and four men whose paths had crossed briefly before all met a violent death.

In Frank Tighe's weak blue eyes there was trepidation. He had the feeling of being caught between the knife and the bullet, and knew with certainty that time was running out.

14

The flutter of his weakening pulse in Ben Stone's ears and the harsh rasp of his own breathing so occupied his world that at first the quiet murmur of approaching hoofbeats went unnoticed.

Then, from the shelter of the pines his horse whickered, jerking Ben out of a half doze. An answering whinny came from behind him, followed by the crackle of breaking chaparral. Inside his chest his heart began to hammer.

Whoever it was, he was climbing from the south end of the canyon. One rider, moving without caution.

They know I'm winged, Ben thought with bitterness. Saw the Henry fall. Kane figures there's no need to send more than one killer after a wounded old man who was fool enough to drop his rifle.

Cold sweat beaded his brow as he

twisted his neck in an effort to look back past the edge of the trees and down the slope. The agony of his torn thigh wrenched a groan from his pale lips. He wrapped an arm around the sticky trunk of the pine, wriggled his body around on the loose needles, clenched his teeth as the sweat trickled into his eyes.

Through blurred eyes Ben saw movement against the skyline. The rider had emerged from thick scrub and was pushing his horse up the grassy slope between the band of scree below the cliffs and the high flat ledge from where Ben had blazed away at Django Orr. As Ben poked a finger inside his spectacles to rub his eyes he saw the rider angle towards him and knew that his horse's greeting had been heard. A sudden surge of helpless rage dragged a bitter oath from between his clenched teeth.

Then his eyesight cleared, and he recognized the rider.

'Christ, it's Young Fox,' he mumbled, and he closed his eyes in horror as he remembered the glittering knife that had leaped from its sheath to threaten Django Orr in the Hangdog Saloon. With a muffled groan he fell back on the pine needles, his body overcome by weakness.

As if in a dream Ben Stone listened to every pin-sharp sound as the horseman drew near. He heard the soft grunt of surprise; the whisper of the Indian's buckskin leggings as he slid from the horse's back; the regular brush of moccasins across pine needles that was suddenly stilled.

Ben stopped breathing.

Warm air stirred against his cheek. A knee nudged his side. Then a firm dry hand touched his face, the hard fingers moving to search for the pulse in his throat.

Ben opened his eyes, drew a ragged breath, instinctively tried to inch away from Young Fox.

Bending over him, the Indian smiled and shook his head. 'You're OK,' he said. 'Though I ain't acted like it so far,

I'm a friendly redskin.' And as Ben sagged weakly, Young Fox looked down at the bloody cloths wrapped around Ben's wounded thigh and reached behind him to the sheath and drew his big knife.

★ ★ ★

When John Gray reached the point where Long Arrow had disappeared he saw at once that the big boulder was not what it seemed. A hundred yard section of the canyon's rimrock had split. Over the centuries the crack had widened and deepened so that a vast wall of rock was left standing parallel to the canyon's side. As Wyoming's extreme weather eroded the outer wall, the bottom of the split gradually filled with compacted detritus. In time the level rose, and the split became an enclosed trail whose northern end was level with the canyon's rim from where it sloped steeply down towards the top edge of the scree.

'From the bottom it'll look like just another crack in the cliffs,' Adam Flint said at Gray's shoulder.

'If we're still in one piece when we get down there.'

But far from being a deadly drop off the cliff edge, the ground on the inner edge of the split had crumbled away allowing easy entry. With a muttered, 'Well, here goes nothing,' Adam Flint kneed his horse past John Gray and across the crumbled lip, and as he entered the shadowy split he immediately saw Long Arrow working his way down some fifty feet below.

The drop was steep, the air uncomfortably cold and dank. Seeping rain water issued from countless fissures to collect and stream down the uneven floor of the split, but still the ground afforded good footing for the horses.

The rattle of hooves echoed in Flint's ears as, behind him, Gray and Baxter gingerly entered the chasm. Then he was concentrating on the way ahead, leaning back against the cantle as his cow pony picked its way down the slope, his knees sometimes brushing the streaming rock walls on either side as the split narrowed.

Ahead of him, sunlight blazed. A dark shape passed through it as Long Arrow left the hidden trail, and Flint heard the rattle of falling stones as the Indian's pony began crossing the loose scree.

Then Adam Flint was out of the chasm, the sudden light dazzling as he gazed with narrowed eyes over a panorama of dark pines and wide patches of wiry mountain grass leading to rocky ledges and beyond those, in the near distance, the familiar sagging roofs of Haven and the wet shine of the flooded draw.

Long Arrow's lead had been cut; on the treacherous scree even his nimble horse was picking his way with difficulty. But he was still some fifty vertical feet downslope from Flint, and had already dropped below the level of the tallest pines.

That first stand of pines formed a

narrow spit between the scree and an expanse of grass beyond which were more trees and the nearest ledge. From his elevated position Flint could see over the tops of those first trees, and now a shocked exclamation burst from his lips that sent his hand groping towards his booted Winchester.

On the edge of the far trees, a black-haired Indian was down on one knee, bending over a white man half reclining against a pine. As Adam Flint rammed the butt of the rifle into his shoulder and worked the lever to put a shell under the hammer, the white man moved his head and sunlight winked on the twin lenses of spectacles.

Jesus! Flint thought: that's Ben Stone.

In the same instant, the Indian's hand moved to his hip. When it came up there was the dazzling flash as a broad blade caught the sun.

'Damn you!' Adam Flint snarled — and taking rapid aim he squeezed the trigger.

The echoes of the shot rolled like thunder along the face of the cliffs, jerking Long Arrow's head around. Flint held the rifle high, gestured with his left hand. In a single bound Long Arrow's pony was off the scree and galloping furiously towards the tongue of trees.

On the fringe of the far trees an arc of bright steel spun in the air as the bullet slammed into the Indian's back and the knife flew from his hand.

He went down, kicking, and for an instant, over the beat of the racing hooves, Adam Flint thought he heard an agonized cry that could have been a long, drawn out 'Noooo . . . '

Then John Gray and Mort Baxter had reached the bottom of the scar that led down from the rimrock and brought their horses up alongside Flint on the edge of the scree. As Long Arrow skirted the spit of trees and began racing his pony across the grass towards the two prostrate figures, the furious rattle of gunfire came drifting up the canyon through the warm morning air.

15

At the crucial moment, Wilf Gannon discovered to his chagrin that he could use his Winchester only by resting the barrel in the fork of a tree.

From the cover of thick scrub a short way up the canyon's west side from where they could see across the roof of the Hangdog, he and Bonnie Darling watched the outlaws working their way methodically through the town. Dakota Slim cleared the shacks on the east side of the street, Frank Tighe those on the west. They were on foot, leading their horses. At each new hovel they let go the reins and walked over to kick in the dilapidated front door if it hadn't already fallen off its broken hinges, then stepped cautiously inside with pistols cocked ready to check that the littered rooms were empty.

Moses Kane rode slowly down the

centre of the street. His six-gun was in his gloved hand. His head swung to left and right as his henchmen went about their work. If Wilf Gannon somehow burst past Slim or Tighe, Kane was there to gun him down — only, Wilf thought with amusement, I ain't there, and if I was I'd bust out through the back door and what'd you do about that, Mister Kane?

'Three of 'em,' Gannon whispered, and in Bonnie Darling's eyes as she listened to those words there was a hint of satisfaction.

'We heard several shots. I'd like to think John took that black-garbed villain with him.'

Then both of them jumped as a shot cracked out. Frank Tighe tumbled backwards out of a shack just up from the Stone's rooming-house, a six-gun smoking in his fist.

As Kane swung towards him and Dakota Slim burst out of the house on the opposite side of the street Wilf heard Tighe's faint shout.

'Rattlesnake,' Wilf mocked, and spat his contempt as Dakota Slim's laughter rang out.

Then Wilf clamped his jaw shut, and his eyes narrowed.

The street widened considerably at the point bordered by the Hangdog and the mercantile to the west, the rooming-house and livery stable to the east. Wilf and Bonnie had already decided that if they opened fire when Kane and his cronies reached that section, the outlaws would have further to run for cover.

'Although,' Wilf said grimly, 'I don't intend to leave any one of 'em on their feet.'

'Almost there,' Bonnie called softly. She had moved a few yards away from Wilf and settled herself behind a thick oak. The Winchester was held loose in her hands, ready to be snapped to her shoulder. The Greener rested against the tree.

And now the voices of the outlaws came clearly to them. The two flank men had reached the part of town that boasted plankwalks, and their boots began to echo hollowly on the flimsy board flooring. Dakota Slim was still in view, but Tighe was now hidden by the mercantile and the Hangdog Saloon.

'Hell!' Gannon swore. 'Hadn't reckoned on those two bastards keeping in tight to the buildings. But both of us have got clear shots at Kane and Slim, and that might be enough.'

And it was then that Wilf tried to lift his rifle and his wounded left arm protested with a fiery bolt of agony.

He yelped, then gritted his teeth and turned to Bonnie and said tightly, 'Holy double goddamn!' just as she lifted the Winchester to her shoulder and squeezed the trigger.

Maybe his squawk of pain distracted her.

Or maybe Moses Kane's horse jinked sideways.

Bonnie pulled her shot. The slug screamed over Kane's head and sent sharp splinters flying from the opposite plankwalk almost under Dakota Slim's feet. Levering fast and skilfully, Bonnie fired four more rapid shots. But even as she did so Kane roared in fury, loosed two wild shots from his six-gun that gouged chunks of bark from the tree sheltering Bonnie, then ducked low and spurred his horse towards the cover of the Hangdog.

At the same time Dakota Slim's half blind gaze searched the hillside as he leaped off the plankwalk and sprinted for his slowly walking horse. He grabbed the horn and swung into the saddle then wrenched the reins tight to spin the horse hard and ride madly towards the alley alongside the saloon.

Confused by the two diverging targets, Bonnie bit her lip hard and sent all four shots slamming into timber walls or digging up gouts of mud from the street.

Wilf had finally got his Winchester wedged in the fork of a tree. With Kane already out of sight he swung on Dakota Slim. In the split second he had left before the outlaw entered the alley he triggered one shot that whistled close enough to send the gunman's battered Stetson flying.

And from almost directly below them they heard a wild yell and timber splintering followed by the musical tinkle of breaking plates and glasses. Moses Kane had spurred his horse up onto the plankwalk and straight through the swing doors into the saloon and was scattering chairs and tables and the remains of breakfast.

The street was clear and silent.

Bonnie Darling moaned softly, furiously, 'Messed it up, Wilf, messed it up,' and in three long, limping strides the old man was by her side, gripping her arm, shaking her.

'Forget that,' he said fiercely. 'Kane'll be coming out the back door. The others'll take the flanks, be like squeezing us in a pincer. So we back off, find cover, lie low. You bring the Greener — '

'No, we can pick them off from here — '

'Tried that already,' he snapped. 'Hit and run's what we we agreed on — '

'Wilf . . . ' She looked into his grey eyes, shook her head. 'You're too darn weary to play soldiers, old friend, we must stick together — '

She broke off as, for a second time, they heard the tinkle of shattering glass. The black barrel of a rifle poked through the mercantile's kitchen window. The muzzle belched flame. Bonnie ducked back as a slug thumped into the tree. A cry was wrenched from her lips as a second whanged off the Winchester's barrel. As the bullet whined into the trees her wrist snapped back and the rifle was ripped from her hands.

Then Wilf's iron grip was back on her arm.

'The shotgun!' he yelled.

Lips tight with pain, Bonnie reached down and grabbed the Greener by its blued barrels. Then, as she hesitated,

Kane blasted two more shots from the kitchen and slugs ripped perilously close through the branches.

'All right,' Wilf said quickly, 'we stay together — but let's get out of here!'

Thirty yards up the hill there were the remains of an old claim, where spoil from the diggings had long ago been transformed by grass and undergrowth into a natural-looking hillock. Wilf knew there would be a deep hollow behind it and, still clinging to Bonnie's arm, he started scrambling up the hill.

The slope was steep and uneven, after the heavy rains made even more difficult and treacherous by mud, loose stones and wet leaves. Grunting with effort, Wilf climbed ten yards, slipping a jolting step back for every two he progressed. Each slip jarred his game hip; each time he flung out an arm to steady himself the agony of his wound made his head swim. And over the rasp of his tortured breathing he could now hear the clatter of hooves and the sound of a horse blowing hard as Dakota Slim emerged from the alley.

'Tighe'll come at us . . . from the other side,' Wilf gasped, and as a loose stone shifted under his boot and he began to slide, he half turned in desperation.

Then Bonnie had impatiently shaken off his grip and moved up close behind him. A firm hand thumped into the small of his back. Her strong legs thrust upwards. Caught by surprise, Wilf found his boots stuck fast in the mud as his body was propelled forwards. He fell on his face in the dirt, came up onto his hands and knees only to be hit by a second shove that drove him further up the slope.

In that way, Bonnie pushing one handed, Wilf scrambling mostly on all fours, they made it to the old diggings. In a whirl of flying limbs and saddle-guns they tumbled over the mound to lie panting in a dip where rank wet grass covered a mossy litter of decaying timber props and rusted shovels.

'Remember the Alamo,' Wilf croaked. He leaned over to spit out what felt like a mouthful of wet soil, reached up to feel the fresh wet blood on his arm then looked across to see Bonnie already wriggling back to the crest of the mound.

'See 'em?'

'You were right. Tighe's working his way round to the south. Slim's horse is there, but . . . '

'He'll be afoot. Must've left his horse, comin' fast through the trees — '

From thick brush thirty yards away gunpowder flamed and a shot blasted, knocking Bonnie Darling backwards off her feet. She landed heavily, cracking her head on moss-covered timbers. The shotgun flew from her hands as a second slug thumped into the mound, kicking a shower of dirt in Wilf's face. He cursed and stumbled back, pawing at his eyes, snapped a blind, one-handed shot from the Winchester that screamed into the sky then tossed the rifle aside and dug clumsily at his hip for his six-gun.

Dimly through the pandemonium he thought he heard the beat of an approaching horse, pulled his scattered wits together to find the source and reckoned despairingly that he'd guessed wrong: Dakota Slim had ridden his horse clear up the slope and was coming at them with guns blazing, there was no way he could be stopped, they were done for . . .

Then Frank Tighe opened up behind them. Hot lead hissed through the air, clipping twigs, thunking into tree trunks, slugs buzzing like angry hornets within inches of Wilf's head. And as Bonnie Darling groaned and rolled over, Moses Kane's mocking laughter rang out from the saloon.

'Got 'em!' he yelled. 'Goddammit, you've got 'em, Slim — '

The kitchen door crashed open at his kick.

Brush crackled all around them as Dakota Slim and Frank Tighe leaped from cover and closed in.

Wilf Gannon threw himself down, crawled through the mouldering leaves to Bonnie Darling. Her hand came up, softly, tremblingly touched his. Through gritty, watering eyes he looked down at her blood-smeared face, the soft dark eyes now filled with pain and sadness. Then, with noise and the stink of gunpowder all around him, he lifted his pistol, cocked it, and prepared to die.

⋆　⋆　⋆

'Jesus Christ!' Adam Flint said, agony in his voice as he reached the trees and reined in. 'I've killed Young Fox.'

'A bloodthirsty rogue Indian, Adam,' Mort Baxter said, his voice puzzled as he brought his horse to a halt. 'If you hadn't plugged him, seems like he'd've slit that feller's throat then taken his scalp.'

'No, this is an Indian wouldn't do that,' Flint said, and his eyes appeared glazed with shock as he flashed a glance at Baxter. 'Young Fox is Long Arrow's son.'

'The kid was fixing to tend to my wound,' Ben Stone said hoarsely, struggling to prop himself up on his elbows. 'Pulled his knife to cut off the bandages.'

Another distant shot was like a twig snapping, coming faintly to their ears from the direction of Haven. From a little way off John Gray called, 'If we're going to do anything for the rest of them, we'd better move, Adam.'

Flint acknowledged the warning with a wave. Almost pleadingly he said, 'What the hell was Young Fox doing here in the canyon, Long Arrow?'

'Came with Kane,' Long Arrow said woodenly. He had stripped the faded blue blanket from his pony and was carefully folding it on the ground. 'Followed him for months, down through Colorado. Must have planted an idea in that killer's mind, brought him here to Haven, figuring to kill him in the same house he took Smooth Skin

228

. . . Didn't think what Kane's coming would mean for the old folks living here . . . '

'Adam!' John Gray shouted.

'All right, Goddammit!' Flint yelled.

Mort Baxter kneed his horse, began to move away.

'Long Arrow . . . ' Flint said helplessly.

'I will stay,' the old Indian said. 'My son is dead. I must sing his death song.'

Flint clamped his lips, watched the Indian kneel down in the centre of the blanket; saw the heavy lids come down over the liquid dark eyes and the seamed face turn up towards the sun's warm rays; heard the first keening, haunting notes of the song that would go on to tell of Young Fox's life — then he put spurs to his horse and headed after Baxter and Gray.

The three men hammered down the hillside at breakneck pace, leaving the route to their horses, mostly hanging on with both hands as wiry scrub threatened to tear them from the saddle and thick overhanging branches put them in danger of decapitation.

At the bottom of the steep slope they thundered through a narrow draw and shot out onto the trail and set off at a gallop, Flint now leading. Half a mile further on, in passing, he glanced fleetingly into the cemetery, saw two horses grazing up near the pines, four bodies lying on the grass, and he wondered sadly who the hell was left for them to rescue.

Then they were thundering through the town's outskirts, their horses' hooves kicking up clods of drying mud. As they swooped down the long slope and the peeling façade of the Hangdog Saloon loomed up, Adam Flint leaped from the saddle and hit the ground running as another fierce rattle of shots was followed by a hoarse bellow of laughter.

Flint went fast into the saloon, a last glance up the street telling him that John Gray's horse had gone lame and his foreman had dropped some way behind. Then, as Mort Baxter lumbered in after him, Flint blinked in the gloom and began kicking his way towards the rear of the saloon through a jumble of splintered tables. A big blue roan with heavy gunny sacks hung behind the saddle panicked at the noise, whickered shrilly and shied out of Flint's way, crashed into the cold iron stove and sent the flue clattering to the floor in billowing clouds of soot.

Choking, spitting, Flint charged past.

'There's your missing cash, Mort!' he yelled, gesturing towards the trembling roan.

Then, drawing his six-gun, he hit a second door with his shoulder, pounded through the empty kitchen and out through the gaping back door.

* * *

The shot, when it came, was from the direction of the kitchen, and for an instant Wilf Gannon, pistol thrust out before him, thought Moses Kane wanted the killing all to himself and was blasting away as he scrambled up the slope.

Then Frank Tighe, on the lip of the hollow and about to plant a slug in the helpless Bonnie Darling, grunted low down in his throat. His pale blue eyes went blank. He reeled backwards, arms weakly flailing, then fell with a crash into the scrub.

Bonnie was the first to realize what was happening.

'Someone's come, Wilf!' she gasped, and a surge of hope brought a choking lump into Gannon's throat.

Then Moses Kane leaped into the hollow, a fearsome, wild-eyed figure, his face set in a savage grin. Instinctively, Wilf recoiled. His finger tightened on the trigger. The six-gun bucked in his fist. The slug nicked Kane's ear. Bright blood showered the outlaw's shoulder. Snarling, Kane kicked out wildly. His boot connected with Gannon's right wrist. A bone cracked and the six-gun fell from nerveless fingers.

But instead of blasting him into

eternity, Gannon was stunned to see Kane turn away, duck down and commence triggering his six-gun in the direction of the saloon.

Off to one side, Dakota Slim was doing the same, backing into the trees as a hail of lead raked the woods.

Bent over, using his left hand to scrabble for the fallen pistol among the wet leaves, Wilf saw Bonnie Darling struggle to her knees. Her hair was matted with mud and leaves. The side of her shirt was soaked with blood. She threw her arms back, coiled her body like a spring, a solid hunk of wood grasped in both hands. Face set, grunting with effort, she swung the length of wood like an axe in a wide, flat arc. There was a meaty thump as it slammed into Kane's shoulder. He roared in pain, half fell sideways. Then, as Wilf's fingers located slippery metal and he fumbled for the six-gun's butt, Kane pushed away from the bank and leaped across the hollow towards Bonnie Darling.

'Come on, come on!' Gannon muttered. He lifted the six-gun out of the wet leaves, but his right hand still wouldn't work. Groaning in frustration, he switched hands; agony from the wound in his upper arm prevented his left thumb from cocking the pistol. Shaking with the effort, he tried to hold the six-gun steady in his left hand and cock the stiff action with the heel of his numb right hand.

But even as he gritted his teeth and felt the hammer click back, he knew he was too late.

John Gray had come around the side of the Hangdog and loped up the easier gradient like a lean timber wolf, an elusive target threading his way through the trees. He shouted a warning, waited until Dakota Slim turned his milky gaze on him then slammed the tall outlaw back into the trees with a single aimed shot in the chest.

As Dakota Slim fell to Gray's accurate shooting, Baxter and Adam Flint were struggling to clamber

234

straight up the steepest part of the slope towards the hollow. It was Baxter who had downed Tighe. Now, while Flint clawed his way upwards, he planted his feet squarely and sent a rain of .45 slugs hissing through the grass on the hollow's lip.

Higher up the slope, Flint roared breathlessly, 'Hold it, Mort!' He had seen Kane close with Bonnie Darling, and Baxter's shots were now putting the brave woman's life in danger.

The noise of gunfire died away. Sensing that the advantage was now his, Moses Kane pounced on Bonnie Darling. He crooked his left arm around her throat and pulled her hard up against his chest, then swung about so that she was between him and the advancing gunmen. Using her body as a shield he dug his heels in and dragged her out of the hollow.

Wilf Gannon's finger was already squeezing the trigger.

The bullet drilled into the crook of Kane's right arm, tore through the elbow and almost spun him off his feet. His six-gun flew high and bounced down the slope. Bonnie caught hold of a wrist and wrenched the outlaw's left arm from her throat. As she fell back, choking, she delivered a fierce, back-hand blow with her clenched fist, sending Kane tumbling backwards into the scrub.

Adam Flint reached the front of the hollow just as John Gray leaped in from the far side. Mort Baxter was having trouble making the climb and had turned to move fast across the slope towards where Kane had fallen. As Bonnie sank to her knees, Flint and Baxter sprang past her. But when they reached the end of the hollow they were met by a hail of bullets and were forced to drop flat and lie gasping, hugging the long grass.

'Firing left-handed, with his second pistol,' Flint panted. 'I thought we had him, but it looks like he's got us pinned down.'

'Yeah, but Mort's got a clear run,'

Gray said breathlessly.

'No. I think he's in trouble,' Wilf Gannon said.

Again he crawled across to Bonnie Darling, eased her back to a comfortable reclining position, tenderly wiped the blood from her face, gingerly touched her side. But the blood on her shirt was already stiffening. 'Bullet went through,' she said. 'I'll live, Wilf.'

John Gray wriggled to the front of the hollow, peered over the edge, said softly, 'Thank the Lord!'

As his words died away they all heard the crackle of brush, fast fading, as Moses Kane made his escape.

'Baxter's down by the saloon,' John Gray said. 'He's taken a slug, but he waved so I reckon he's OK.'

Adam Flint turned and slid heavily to a sitting position in the hollow, his long legs crossed. He ripped off his hat, used his forearm to scrub the sweat from his brow.

'Just you two down here, Wilf?'

'Jenny Stone's hid up in the hills.'

Wilf glanced at Bonnie, hesitating, and she said, 'My husband, John, was taken up to the cemetery with Hank Travis to bury our town constable.'

'I'm sorry, ma'am,' Flint said awkwardly. 'I saw four bodies when I rode past.'

Wilf Gannon frowned. 'Three are ours. Tighe and Slim're here, both of 'em dead. Kane's on the loose. That leaves Django Orr and the Injun.'

'I guess Orr's one of those in the cemetery,' Flint said. 'I shot the Indian up in the hills. He's there now with Ben Stone. Ben's shot up, but he'll pull through. Long Arrow's singing a death song.' He paused, said quietly, 'The Indian I plugged was Young Fox. He was Long Arrow's son.'

Wilf Gannon's eyes widened. 'That kid with them outlaws? I knew Long Arrow had a son, but I ain't never seen him.'

'Been hunting Kane for a while. Seems he talked him into coming here,' John Gray said. 'Had some notion of killing him in his old house.'

'Poetic justice,' Bonnie Darling said. 'But in the end, Kane got away.'

'I could go after him,' Wilf Gannon said. There was hesitation in his voice, and Bonnie smiled.

'No. With John gone I need some- body to help clear up the saloon . . . '

Wilf grinned sadly. 'And run the mercantile, take care of Hank's stable, maybe in my spare time take on the small job of town constable.'

'It's all go, Wilf,' Adam Flint said climbing wearily to his feet. 'But before you get down to work there's wounds to be dressed, and as Haven ain't got a doctor . . . '

* * *

Long Arrow brought Ben Stone down from the hills for an emotional reunion with Jenny when the autumn sun was already an hour down below the western rim of High Falls Canyon.

Wilf Gannon did dress Ben's

wounds, as he did those of Mort Baxter and Bonnie Darling, applying a modicum of skill but an awful lot of the compassion that came naturally to those fine characters who had frequented the Hangdog Saloon.

And later that same day, of his own volition, he took Dan Ford's tarnished badge from the body of the dead outlaw, Dakota Slim, and pinned it to his own shirt front.

Two days later, Long Arrow rode out through Twin Bluffs Pass with Adam Flint, John Gray and Mort Baxter, who had his left arm in a sling, two heavy gunny-sacks tied back of his saddle and a smile never far from his face.

A mile beyond the pass, at the end of the arroyo where the floodwaters began their spread across the buffalo grass, the four men found the body of Moses Kane. The way they figured it, after he had crashed through the brush away from the hollow behind the Hangdog he must have doubled back and caught the nearest horse wandering loose in

Haven's main street, then tried to make it through the Twin Bluffs Pass.

That horse had been John Gray's.

Lame in its left hind leg, it had been unable to negotiate the ledge that was the only possible way through the still flooded pass; the canyon that had expelled Moses Kane once, without violence, this time tumbled him like a limp rag doll against the jagged rocks and left him to die on the plains.

THE END

We do hope that you have enjoyed reading this large print book.

Did you know that all of our titles are available for purchase?

We publish a wide range of high quality large print books including:
Romances, Mysteries, Classics
General Fiction
Non Fiction and Westerns

Special interest titles available in large print are:
The Little Oxford Dictionary
Music Book, Song Book
Hymn Book, Service Book

Also available from us courtesy of Oxford University Press:
Young Readers' Dictionary
(large print edition)
Young Readers' Thesaurus
(large print edition)

For further information or a free brochure, please contact us at:
Ulverscroft Large Print Books Ltd.,
The Green, Bradgate Road, Anstey,
Leicester, LE7 7FU, England.
Tel: (00 44) **0116 236 4325**
Fax: (00 44) **0116 234 0205**